THE TIPSTER

A mysterious man calling himself 'the Tipster' telephones the *Daily Clarion* newspaper and announces his intention to commit five murders, beginning with Lord Latimer, Senior Steward of the Jockey Club. John Tully, News Editor of the *Daily Clarion*, believes the call to be a hoax by a madman — until Lord Latimer is shot dead while walking in the grounds of his house at Newbury. Superintendent Budd of Scotland Yard is called to investigate; but his powers are put to the test as several more people are brutally murdered . . .

GERALD VERNER

THE TIPSTER

Complete and Unabridged

LINFORD
Leicester

First published in Great Britain

First Linford Edition
published 2018

*All the characters in this story are
entirely fictitious*

*A catalogue record for this book is available
from the British Library.*

ISBN 978–1–4448–3701–8

To
DAVID H. GODFREY
AND
ALL CONCERNED IN
PUTTING 'THE TIPSTER'
ON THE AIR

1

The car slowed down, drew into the side of the narrow little street, and stopped. The driver slid from behind the wheel and got out. Whistling softly, he looked quickly up and down the deserted road and then walked towards the scarlet painted call-box that formed a splash of colour against the surrounding drabness.

Still whistling he entered the kiosk, consulted a slip of paper, and producing two pennies from his pocket, lifted the receiver and inserted the coins in the slot. Rapidly he dialled a number and waited.

A girl's voice came over the wire: 'The *Daily Clarion*.'

The man in the call-box stopped whistling and pressed the button marked 'A.' He said, speaking in a queer nasal drawl that was reminiscent of the late but un-lamented Lord Haw-Haw: 'I want to speak to the News Editor.'

'One moment, please,' said the switchboard girl, and he waited while he was put through, watching through the glass for any signs of life in the still deserted street with wary, restless eyes.

'News Editor, *Daily Clarion*,' said a crisp voice curtly.

'I have some information for you — exclusive information,' said the man in the call-box in his unnatural nasal whine. 'It is my intention to commit five murders . . . '

An exclamation from the listener at the other end of the telephone interrupted him.

'*What* did you say?' demanded the startled News Editor.

'I said it was my intention to commit five murders,' the man in the call-box continued calmly. 'I shall begin with Lord Latimer, Senior Steward of the Jockey Club . . . '

'Look here, are you mad?' snapped the News Editor angrily. 'Or is this your idea of a joke?'

'Neither, I assure you,' said the man in the call-box. 'I intend to kill Lord Latimer first. The names of the other four persons concerned I will communicate to you before each — er — shall we call it — event?'

'What the devil are you talking about?' exclaimed the News Editor irritably. 'Who *are* you?'

'Prudence compels me to withhold my real identity,' replied the caller coolly, 'but, since you will be hearing from me quite frequently in the near future, I suppose I ought to give you some sort of pseudonym for reference? How about . . . the Tipster? That seems to be appropriate, don't you think? The Tipster . . . '

He hung up the receiver in the midst of the News Editor's frantic flood of questions, left the call-box and walked slowly back to his car, softly resuming his gentle whistling of Debussy's 'Clair de Lune' as he got in and drove rapidly away.

II

John Tully, News Editor of that enterprising newspaper the *Daily Clarion*, wiped his perspiring brow and glared at Dowling, his chief sub.

'Either the fellow's stark, raving mad, or trying to put over a hoax,' he growled. 'I should think the latter was more likely. Nasty sort of voice, though — like that blasted fellow Haw-Haw's . . . '

'Bit of a racing fan by the sound of it, J.T.,' remarked Dowling, rubbing the bald spot on the top of his head gently. 'Calling himself the Tipster and picking on Lord Latimer, Senior Steward of the Jockey Club . . . '

'Then why the devil couldn't he have rung up the Sports Editor instead of damn-well bothering me?' grunted Tully. He picked up a sheaf of papers from his huge, littered desk. 'Here's Coleman's speech. Take it and cut it down to half a column. If the Government cut our newsprint they can't grumble if we have to cut their speeches . . . '

'O.K., J.T.,' said the rotund Mr. Dowling, and then hesitantly: 'I say . . . you don't think there might be something in it?'

'There's *never* anything in Coleman's speeches,' snapped Tully, pushing his horned-rimmed spectacles up on to his forehead and rubbing his eyes.

'I mean this 'Tipster' business,' explained Dowling. 'If he's a maniac he may be dangerous?'

'I think he's some fool trying to be funny,' said the News Editor. 'If I thought for a moment he was serious . . . '

'That's just the point, J.T.,' persisted Dowling. 'Supposing he *is*? Don't you think we ought to warn the police?'

'H'm . . . ' Tully frowned and pulled gently at his big nose. 'Yes . . . I suppose we ought. Latimer lives at Newbury, I think. Make certain and notify the local police. I still think it's a hoax, though . . . '

He reached for the house phone and began talking rapidly to the chief compositor, and Dowling, recognizing that the subject was closed, went away to look up Lord Latimer's address and inform the local police of the threat which the unknown had uttered against that august individual's life.

The Newbury police, in the person of a rather gruff-voiced desk-sergeant, were not very interested. It seemed that they shared John Tully's opinion that the thing was a hoax. They promised, however, to notify Lord Latimer of what had occurred.

All this began at nine o'clock on a very hot summer's night in the middle of June and at half-past eleven John Tully and the Newbury police realized that they were wrong. The message from the man calling himself the Tipster was anything but a hoax, for, at eleven o'clock, Lord Latimer was shot dead while walking in the grounds of his house at Newbury, and the murderer escaped without leaving behind any tangible clue to his identity.

III

Superintendent Budd became involved in the affair almost exactly an hour after he had arrived at Scotland Yard on the following morning. He was sitting in his cheerless office smoking one of his evil-smelling black cigars and wondering how he was going to cope with the abnormal heat-wave, under which London was slowly grilling, when the house telephone uttered its warning buzz, and he was requested to go down to the Assistant Commissioner's office at once.

With a sigh he laid down his half-smoked cigar on the ashtray, rose ponderously to his feet and slowly resumed his jacket. He had just completed a difficult case of fraud which had needed a great deal of labour and he had been hoping for an interval of comparative leisure. But it seemed that this was not to be. He made his way without enthusiasm to Colonel Blair's office and knocked with a pudgy hand. The Assistant Commissioners' voice curtly bade him come in, and he entered.

Colonel Blair, as immaculate and dapper as usual, in spite of the heat, was sitting behind his large desk, rolling a pencil between his manicured fingers.

'Sit down, Superintendent,' he greeted, nodding towards a chair.

Mr. Budd walked over and lowered his portly form gently into the protesting chair. He waited while the Assistant Commissioner consulted some notes on a slip of paper on his blotting-pad.

'I've had a request,' he began after a

7

pause, 'from the Chief Constable of the Berkshire County Police for assistance. There was a murder last night at Newbury. Lord Latimer was shot dead in the grounds of his house . . . '

'Lord Latimer?' murmured Mr. Budd. 'Isn't — er — wasn't 'e somethin' ter do with racin', sir?'

'Yes, he was Senior Steward of the Jockey Club.' Colonel Blair nodded his neat grey head. 'The details I've got here are pretty meagre but no doubt the local people will be able to augment them quite a lot. I hope so. The murder was committed at eleven o'clock last night. It appears that Latimer, when the night was warm enough, invariably smoked a cigar in his grounds before going to bed. The butler, who had just come in from his evening off, heard the shot and went to investigate. He found his master lying on a path near a belt of shrubbery, quite dead, with a bullet wound in his head. There was no sign of the killer but the butler states that, as he left the house, he heard somebody whistling . . . '

'Ardly likely to've been the murderer,

sir,' remarked Mr. Budd. ''E wouldn't want to draw attention to 'imself . . . '

Colonel Blair looked at him thoughtfully.

'I wouldn't be too sure of that,' he said. 'The murderer seems to be rather partial to publicity. Apparently he rang up the News Editor of the *Daily Clarion* at nine o'clock last night — two hours before the crime was actually committed — and told him what he was going to do . . . '

The usually phlegmatic Mr. Budd was startled.

''E did *what*, sir?' he exclaimed.

'Incredible, isn't it?' said the Assistant Commissioner. 'But it's a fact. He stated that he was going to kill Lord Latimer and four other people whose names he didn't mention. Quite naturally, the News Editor thought the whole thing was a hoax. He had the Newbury police notified, however, and they sent a man to warn Latimer. He took the same view as Tully, the News Editor . . . '

'Did 'e give any name, this feller, when he rang up?' asked Mr. Budd sleepily.

'Yes, he called himself the Tipster,' answered Colonel Blair. 'Quite appropriate, in view

9

of what's happened, eh? The front page of the *Clarion* this morning features the story . . . Haven't you seen it?'

'I never read the *Clarion*, sir,' said Mr. Budd disparagingly.

Colonel Blair smiled.

'Neither do I, as a rule,' he declared. 'I should read it this morning, though, if I were you. None of the other newspapers has got the story yet. Well, that's about all I can tell you. You'd better get away to Newbury at once. Superintendent Pollard of the local police, is in charge of the inquiry and he'll give you any other details they've got . . . '

Mr. Budd recognized that this was his dismissal and got carefully to his feet.

'I'll take Sergeant Leek with me, sir,' he said, and went to find the melancholy Leek and acquaint him with the result of his interview.

IV

The little car sped along the country road leaving a trail of dust in its wake. Looking at it few people would have believed that it was capable of such a speed, but the engine beneath its ancient radiator had been a good one in its day and still possessed remnants of its pristine glory.

The girl who sat beside the driver, her dark hair blowing in the breeze, broke a long silence.

'Of all the crazy things you've ever done, Gordon,' she said, 'this is the craziest — and that's saying something.'

'Oh, is it,' answered the young man at the wheel, without taking his eyes off the road ahead. 'You just wait and see, Vicky. When the name of Gordon Cross is plastered all over the front page of the *Clarion*, you'll change your tune . . . '

'Rubbish!' she declared stubbornly. 'When we get to Latimer's place they'll just throw us out . . . '

'The trouble with you, Vicky,' he said, 'is you've no confidence in your husband's ability . . . '

'I've yet to see any of it, darling,' she retorted.

'That,' he remarked, 'is a most unwifely statement.'

'If you think that,' she said, 'you don't know much about wives.'

'Don't I?' he answered with a grin. 'Before I married you my experience was vast . . .'

'Don't go into the sordid details of your lurid past, darling,' said his wife. 'It's the present I'm concerned with. What do you expect to gain by this hare-brained scheme?'

'It's not hare-brained,' he exclaimed, indignantly. 'Don't you realize that this is the opportunity of a lifetime?'

'No, I don't,' she interrupted.

'Oh, what is the good of trying to talk sense?' he demanded. 'Don't you understand? This Tipster business is going to be a big thing. It's going to appeal to the public's imagination. If I can find out what's behind it — get the inside story — I can make the *Clarion* give me a job . . .'

'Hasn't it occurred to you, my poor deluded darling,' said Vicky, 'that the *Clarion* will have its own crime man on the job?'

'Jameson?' Gordon Cross laughed scornfully. 'If I can't do better than he I'll

. . . I'll eat my hat . . . '

'You never wear one, darling' she said.

'Oh, do be serious, Vicky,' he expostulated. 'Don't you see . . . '

'I know what you're trying to do, Gordon,' she said in a different tone, 'and I honestly believe you could pull it off — if you had a chance. But what chance are you going to get? We're not exactly going to be welcomed with open arms by the police or the other reporters, or the dead man's relatives. You haven't any standing, darling. You're just a free-lance journalist out of a job . . . They'll chuck us out on our necks . . . '

There was some truth in what she said and he was forced to admit this. It wasn't going to be a walk-over by any manner of means. After all that was all he was — 'a free-lance journalist out of a job' and nobody was going to take very kindly to his butting in . . .

He ran his fingers through his unruly mop of wavy hair. 'Well, you never get anything without trying, and . . . '

'Gordon, look out!' said Vicky, in alarm, and he came back to earth just in time to swerve violently and avoid a man on a bicycle who had suddenly shot out of a side turning. 'You nearly ran him down,' said Vicky, as he straightened the car.

'The idiot shouldn't have popped out suddenly like that,' he answered, 'almost under my front wheels . . . '

'You should have been looking what you were doing, you mean,' answered Vicky. She turned her head and looked back at the cyclist, who was now almost out of sight behind them.

'We're nearly there,' said Gordon suddenly. 'That's Latimer's place . . . '

'Where?' she asked.

'That . . . that big gate on the right . . . '

'How funny,' remarked Vicky, sarcastically. 'It says 'fresh manure, twenty shillings a cartload . . . '

'Oh . . . ' said Gordon, a little disconcerted. 'I must have made a mistake, then.'

She patted his arm soothingly.

'Never mind, my sweet,' she said. 'You do your best.'

For a little while there was silence and then she said thoughtfully: 'Gordon — that man on the bicycle . . . Did you get a good look at him?'

'Can't say I did,' he replied. 'Why?'

'Do you remember when you were doing 'Round the Courts' for the *Sentinel*,' she said, 'a man called Maurice Swayne was brought up for blackmailing somebody or other and got off for lack of evidence?'

'Yes,' he nodded quickly. 'Nasty piece of work. He should have got ten years . . . '

'Well, that was Swayne — on the bicycle,' she said seriously.

'Are you *sure*?' he said incredulously.

'Quite sure, darling,' she answered. 'I can never forget a face — not even yours.'

V

Mr. Budd sat in the sunny morning room at White Gables, Lord Latimer's house at Newbury, looking more sleepy-eyed than usual. Sergeant Leek, the picture of dejection, leaned against the frame of the open french window. Facing them both, by the table, sat Iris Latimer, the dead man's daughter. She was a fair girl with a wealth of honey-coloured hair that she wore in a long page-boy to her shoulders. Slim without being thin, she gave the impression of lithe virility — a girl who would sit a horse well without losing any of her natural femininity. Her face was pale and her eyes were troubled. The tragedy which had come out of the night had left her stunned and hopeless. She looked as though she were just waking from some horrible and fantastic nightmare.

Mr. Budd's manner was wholly sympathetic as he cleared his throat and said, in his deep husky rumble:

'It'ud be a lot of help, miss, if we could get a line on the motive. 'Ad your father any enemies, now?'

She shook her head listlessly. Her voice when she spoke was a little tremulous.

'I can't think of anyone — anyone at all — who would have wished him any harm — not anyone . . . '

'Racin' attracts a queer lot o' people,' said the big man. 'Now Lord Latimer 'eld a pretty high position, didn't 'e? If 'e'd discovered some kind o' swindle say . . . an' was goin' to expose it?'

'I'm sure there was nothing of the kind,' she said. 'He would have told me . . . He always told me everything . . . '

The tears filled her eyes, but she forced them back. Mr. Budd waited until she had recovered her composure before he asked his next question.

''Ave you ever 'eard him mention someone called the Tipster?' he inquired.

'It's a very common term in racing, isn't it?' she answered. 'There are hundreds of tipsters — he never mentioned any particular one . . . '

'The name — it's an alias, of course — don't convey anything to you?'

'I'm afraid it doesn't,' said Iris.

'This butler of yours, Miss Latimer, what's-'is-name — Masters,' went on the stout superintendent, 'states that just after 'e 'eard the shot 'e 'eard somebody whistlin'. Did you 'appen to hear it?'

'I never heard anything,' she replied. 'I

was very tired and I went to bed early — just after ten. I fell asleep at once and I didn't know any . . . anything had happened until my maid woke me . . . '

'Of course,' said Mr. Budd thoughtfully, 'there's a possibility this feller's just a 'omicidal maniac — that seems the more likely explanation . . . '

'He must be,' said Iris. 'Nobody could have had any reason for . . . for killing daddy . . . '

'It's surprisin' what queer thin's crop up when yer investigatin' a case like this, miss,' declared Mr. Budd. ''Ow long 'as this butler o' yours been in your employ?'

'Masters?' She looked at him with a hint of surprise. 'Oh, you're not suggesting . . . '

'No, miss,' said Mr. Budd, 'I'm not suggestin' anythin'. I'm just collectin' all the information I can. 'Ow' long 'as Masters been with you?'

'Just over a year,' she answered. 'Our previous butler was a very old man. He died in our service . . . '

'I see.' Mr. Budd rubbed his chins gently. 'You've always found Masters honest an' trustworthy?'

'Oh, yes,' she said at once. 'Always.'

'Were you present,' continued the big man, 'when the local police informed Lord Latimer that this man — the Tipster — 'ad rung up the *Daily Clarion* an' threatened 'is life?'

'Yes. Daddy laughed and said it must be a stupid joke or else the man was a lunatic.'

'You think his attitude was genuine?' asked Mr. Budd. ' 'E wasn't alarmed an' just tryin' to reassure you?'

'No . . . I'm quite sure he wasn't,' she said.

The big man sighed. It was all very perplexing. There was no clue at all either to the identity of the person who had shot Lord Latimer or the reason why they had done so.

'It's a queer business,' he said. 'You can't think of anything at all, miss, that might 'elp us?'

'I'm afraid I can't . . . ' she began and then her calmness suddenly broke and she burst out: 'It was a cruel, beastly, horrible thing to do . . . '

She stopped suddenly, abruptly, as there came a knock on the door and Masters, the butler, entered.

'Excuse me,' he said. 'Mr. Kenwood is here, miss. I told him you were engaged, but he said he would wait. He's in the drawing-room.'

'Thank you, Masters,' said Iris. She looked at Mr. Budd. 'Is there anything else you want to ask me?'

'Not at present, miss, thank you,' he said. 'I'm sorry to 'ave 'ad to bother you at all in the circumstances.'

'I understand . . . ' She got up and went over to the door which Masters held open for her. 'Please ask for . . . for anything you want . . . '

She went out and the butler was following when Mr. Budd called him back.

'Just a minute, Masters,' he said.

The butler came back and closed the door.

'Yes, sir?' he said inquiringly.

'Who's this Mr. Kenwood?' asked Mr. Budd.

'He's a friend of Miss Latimer's, sir,'

20

answered Masters. 'He lives at Pine Ridge — about a mile away from here.'

'An old friend, is he?'

'Yes, sir, I believe so.'

'Did Lord Latimer an' this feller always get on well together?'

'I think they were on the best of terms, sir.'

'No recent quarrel or anythin' o' the sort?'

'Not to my knowledge, sir.'

Mr. Budd yawned. Outside from the broiling garden came waves of heat and scent.

'It was your evenin' off last night, wasn't it?' asked the big man.

'Yes, sir.'

'What did you do with your time?'

'I went to the pictures, sir.'

'Alone?'

'Yes, sir.'

'What did you see?'

'*The Two Mrs. Carrolls*, sir. I am rather partial to Humphrey Bogart.'

'Did you come straight back here?'

'No, sir. I dropped into the *Compasses* for a drink. I reached here just before eleven. I had hardly come in when I heard the shot . . . '

Sergeant Leek roused himself from his listless position against the window pane. He said:

'None o' the other servants 'eard or saw anythin'. They was all asleep in their beds . . . '

'Where else would yer expect 'em to sleep?' snarled Mr. Budd.

'If you ask me . . . ' began the sergeant.

'I'm not askin' you anythin',' said Mr. Budd irritably. 'If I did you wouldn't be able ter tell me.' He turned to the waiting butler. 'About that time you 'eard somebody whistlin' — just after the shot — what was it?'

'I'm afraid I can't tell you, sir,' said Masters. 'It was a tune I am unfamiliar with . . . '

'Can't you give me some idea? Try whistlin' it yerself . . . '

Masters frowned. He pursed his lips and uttered a few tuneless notes. They conveyed nothing at all to Mr. Budd. The butler was continuing when there came a sudden interruption.

'Budd, by all that's wonderful!' cried a voice from the window, and the big man swung round to see Gordon Cross staring in at them.

'Mr. Cross!' he ejaculated. 'What are you doin' 'ere — sneakin' in by the winder?'

'I wasn't sneaking,' said Gordon indignantly. 'I didn't want to disturb the household so I prowled round, saw this window open and here I am . . . '

'I s'pose,' said Mr. Budd, eyeing him distastefully, 'that you're after a story, eh? What paper are you workin' for now?'

'Owing to the general obtuseness of news editors collectively — none,' said Gordon, coming further into the room. 'I say — what's the idea of the rather unsuccessful attempt to whistle 'Clair de Lune'?'

'Is that what it's called?' asked Mr. Budd quickly.

'Yes.' Cross nodded and looked from one to the other. 'What's the idea?'

'Somebody was 'eard whistlin' that tune just after the shot was fired that killed Lord Latimer,' said Mr. Budd.

23

'Whistling? Whistling 'Clair de Lune'?' asked Gordon.

'Well, that's what *you* say the thin's called,' remarked the big man.

Masters coughed gently.

'Excuse me, sir,' he said. 'If you don't require me any more, I have . . . '

'That's all right, Masters,' interrupted Mr. Budd, and the butler went quietly out.

'Well,' said Gordon Cross, 'I never expected to find *you* here, Budd. What a bit of luck . . . '

'Whose?' demanded Mr. Budd pointedly.

'Mutual, I hope,' said Gordon. 'Now suppose you give me all the details . . . '

'Now see here, Mr. Cross,' began Mr. Budd, with great determination, but he was interrupted by a musical voice which said with cooing sweetness:

'This is a pleasant surprise. How *nice* to see you again, Mr. Budd. And Sergeant Leek, too. Why, it's quite like old times, isn't it?'

Vicky was standing in the window surveying them with a dazzling smile.

Mr. Budd sighed. It was a sigh of resignation.

'You're 'ere as well, are you, Mrs. Cross?' he said wearily.

'Why, of course,' she answered. 'I've been waiting outside because I expected to see Gordon thrown out . . . '

'I'm sorry you were disappointed,' said Mr. Budd with feeling.

'Now you're not going to be difficult, are you?' said Gordon.

'Of course he isn't,' declared Vicky.

'If you think I'm goin' to 'and out information for you two to sell to the newspapers . . . ' began Mr. Budd severely.

'You've got it all wrong,' broke in Gordon. 'We don't want to sell anything to the newspapers — not yet anyway. I think there's a big thing behind this business. This is only the *beginning* of it. I've a hunch the Tipster *means* what he said about those other four people . . . Sooner or later the *Clarion* will get *another* message . . . '

'If that 'appens we'll get him,' said Mr. Budd grimly. 'I've got a man listening in, and . . . '

'I wouldn't be too sure,' remarked Gordon. 'I don't believe you're going to catch him as easily as all that . . . '

'Oh, you don't, eh?' grunted Mr. Budd.

'No,' continued Gordon quickly. 'The usual routine methods aren't going to get you anywhere in this business . . . '

'I suppose,' interrupted Mr. Budd, 'you think you could do better, eh?'

'I'd like to try,' said Gordon eagerly. 'You're up against something right out of the ordinary and you'll need all the help you can get . . . '

'There's still a few fellers left at the Yard, you know,' said Mr. Budd.

'I don't mean that kind of help,' said Gordon. 'Look here, all I want is an opportunity to find out the truth — the *whole* truth. I promise you I won't use any of it without your permission, but I want to be the first with the exclusive story . . . when it *is* published.'

'It can't do any harm, Mr. Budd, can it?' pleaded Vicky; 'and Gordon's quite good at that sort of thing. He did help you a lot with the Bell case, didn't he?'

'H'm.' Mr. Budd remembered the case

to which she referred. Young Cross had been useful — very useful . . . He was a nice chap, too. Had a run of pretty bad luck lately . . .

'Well, Mr. Cross, if you promise you won't go usin' anythin' you find out without my permission . . . '

Gordon Cross gave a delighted whoop.

'It's a bargain!' he said. 'Now tell me all you've got up to date?'

'That's easy,' grunted Mr. Budd. 'Nuthin'.'

'Nothing?' echoed Vicky.

'Somebody shot Latimer last night without leavin' any clue to 'is identity . . . ' said the big man.

'Except that tune,' said Gordon Cross thoughtfully, 'the tune the murderer was heard whistling . . . '

'You can't call that much of a clue,' grunted Mr. Budd.

'I wonder,' murmured Gordon. 'It's a queer thing for a killer to do, isn't it? — just after he's committed a murder . . . '

The stout detective shrugged his massive shoulders.

'We don't even know it *was* the murderer,' he said.

'No.' Gordon Cross scratched his smooth chin gently and stared at Sergeant Leek with half-closed eyes, until that melancholy man began to wriggle uncomfortably. 'No,' he repeated. 'But if it had been anyone else they'd have heard the shot and come to see what had happened, wouldn't they? I think you ought to treat that tune more seriously . . . I've an idea, you know, it's more important than you imagine — much more important . . . '

Mr. Budd was surprised. It was not until very much later that he realized that Gordon Cross had been right.

2

I

The sun beat down relentlessly from a sky that was cloudless, and there was scarcely a breath of wind to stir the leaves of the trees. In the shade of a great cedar, however, where Iris Latimer stood talking to a tall, dark-haired young man, in a light grey flannel suit, it was slightly less hot.

'It's nice out here, David,' said the girl, staring at the shaven lawn with tired eyes. 'After the nightmare of last night and this morning . . . the house full of policemen and reporters . . . and questions, questions, questions . . . It's been horrible . . . You can't imagine how horrible . . . '

'I can, Iris.' David Kenwood's lean dark face was troubled. 'You must be worn out. Why don't you try and get some rest? You can't have had any sleep . . . '

'I haven't,' she replied, 'but I couldn't

rest . . . David, do you think they'll find him — the beast who did it?'

'I'm sure they will,' he said.

'Who could it have been?' She turned towards him and looked up into his face. 'Why should anyone have wanted to kill daddy? He never did anybody any harm . . . '

'It must have been a lunatic, dear,' declared Kenwood. 'That telephone call to the *Daily Clarion* wasn't the action of a sane man . . . '

'But why should he pick on daddy?' she asked. 'And who are the four other people he mentioned?'

'Perhaps there aren't any other people,' he said. 'What do the police think about it?'

'I don't know what they think,' she said frowning. 'They don't seem to be doing much . . . '

'Well, they haven't had much time yet,' he remarked reasonably.

'The man from Scotland Yard doesn't look very clever,' she said. 'He's enormously fat and appears to be half asleep most of the time.'

'I daresay he knows his job,' said Kenwood. 'Most of them are pretty good, you know. They have to be. Very few criminals slip through their fingers.'

'I hope they find him,' said Iris. 'That's all I want — to find him . . . To know that he'll *hang* . . . '

He was startled at the sudden change in her. Her eyes had hardened and her mouth had set . . . Something in her nature that he had never seen or suspected before had thrust its way to the surface, and he didn't altogether like it . . .

'I don't think you ought to stop here all alone brooding over it,' he said. 'Why not come over to Pine Ridge for a week or two? Lydia would be delighted . . . '

She shook her head.

'It's very sweet of you, David, and Lydia too,' she said, 'but I'd rather stop here . . . really . . . '

He saw that it would be useless to press her.

'Well, if you should change your mind the offer's always open,' he said.

The hardness that had come into her face softened and was gone.

'I'll remember that,' she said. 'I haven't thanked you for coming so promptly yet, have I?'

'I'd have been here before only I had to go up to London yesterday, and I didn't get back till late this morning,' he said. 'You know I can hardly believe it yet . . . It seems impossible that . . . '

'There's Masters,' she interrupted him suddenly. 'I think he must be looking for me . . . Yes, he is. What is it, Masters?'

The butler came quickly towards them.

'There's a gentleman called to see you, miss,' he said.

Iris frowned.

'Who is it?' she asked.

'He didn't give his name, miss,' said the butler. 'He's in the drawing-room . . . '

'I suppose I'd better go,' she sighed wearily. 'It's probably only another reporter . . . there have been hordes of them . . . Come with me, David . . . '

They came out of the shadow of the great cedar into the hot sunshine and walked across the smooth grass towards the open french windows of the drawing-room. A piano began to tinkle softly as somebody picked out a melody with one finger. Masters paused and they saw his body stiffen.

'That's the tune, miss,' he whispered, excitedly. 'That's the tune I heard somebody whistling last night . . . '

'Are you *sure?*' asked Iris doubtfully.

'Quite sure, miss,' said the butler.

The melody went on until they reached the windows and then stopped abruptly as they entered the long room. The player was standing by the grand piano. A man of medium height clad in a check suit of a rather loud pattern, with smooth dark hair shining with oil. His voice, when he spoke, matched the oiliness of his hair. He said:

'Miss Latimer? Good morning. And Mr. Kenwood, too. Now isn't that lucky . . . Miss Latimer, allow me to introduce myself. My name is Swayne — Maurice Swayne . . . '

The door of the drawing-room was thrown open suddenly and Mr. Budd came in quickly.

'Who was playin' that tune just now?' demanded the big man sharply.

'Clair de Lune?' inquired Mr. Maurice Swayne blandly. 'One of Debussy's most charming compositions, sir. I'm sure Mr. Kenwood will agree with me . . . won't you, Mr. Kenwood?'

The question was accompanied by a sneering twist of the rather thick lips.

'What the devil, are you doing here, Swayne?' demanded Kenwood angrily. 'I thought . . . ' He swayed a little and his face went suddenly white.

'David — what's the matter?' said Iris anxiously. 'You look ill . . . '

'It's all right,' muttered Kenwood. He passed his hand over his forehead quickly. 'The sun was a . . . a little hot . . . out there . . . '

'Sit down over there — in the shade,' said Iris. 'Masters — fetch Mr. Kenwood a glass of water . . . '

'Yes, miss.' The butler went over to the door, and Gordon Cross and Vicky, who had grouped themselves curiously on the threshold, stood aside for him to pass.

'Are you a friend o' Mr. Kenwood's, sir?' inquired Mr. Budd.

Maurice Swayne turned towards him

with a bland smile.

'Well — er — hardly a friend,' he said, in his rich oily voice. 'Shall we say a business acquaintance? I must apologize, Miss Latimer, for intruding at such a time, but I am the possessor of certain information which I feel it is my duty . . . in the circumstances . . . '

'What sort of information, sir?' said Mr. Budd curtly.

Mr. Swayne surveyed him speculatively.

'Are you the officer in charge of the — er — investigation into Lord Latimer's tragic — er — demise?' he asked politely.

'Yes,' said the big man, 'I'm Sup'n'tendent Budd, C.I.D. New Scotland Yard . . . '

'Ah!' Maurice Swayne nodded and rubbed his soft hands gently together. 'Then, of course, you are the fellow I should see. I have been staying for the past few days in Newbury on holiday — I have a room at the *Compasses* — a delightful inn . . . charming in every way . . . ' He paused as Masters came back with a glass of water on a tray, which he took over to David Kenwood.

'Go on, sir,' grunted Mr. Budd. 'What's this information you're talkin' about?'

'I'm coming to that,' said Maurice Swayne. It was evident that he was thoroughly enjoying himself and had no intention of being hurried. 'I have been in the habit of taking long walks round the district before going to bed — I find the exercise beneficial to sleep. Last night, just after eleven, I was in the vicinity of this house . . . '

He paused, dramatically, surveying his audience to see the reaction to his words.

'I s'pose,' remarked Mr. Budd, 'you 'eard the shot an' somebody whistlin' that tune you was playin'?'

'Oh, yes,' said Mr. Swayne. 'Yes, I did. But I did more than that — er — Superintendent. *I saw the murderer!*'

II

'Gin and orange for you, Vicky?' said Gordon Cross.

'Please,' answered his wife. 'Gordon's if they have it.'

'What's yours, Budd?'

'Pint o' beer, please, Mr. Cross,' said

Mr. Budd. He looked sleepily round the bar of the *Compasses*. 'Nice pub,' he murmured.

'Two pints of bitter and a Gordon's gin and orange,' said Cross to the languid girl behind the bar.

'Only mild and bitter — sorry,' she said indifferently.

'All right, that'll do,' said Gordon.

'There's a table over there,' said Vicky. 'Shall we go over?'

'Yes — you grab it,' said Gordon . . . 'We'll bring the drinks . . . '

She went over to the table and presently they joined her with the drinks.

'Not a bad drop o' beer that,' remarked Mr. Budd, setting down his tankard after a long draught.

'Pretty good,' agreed Gordon. 'A lot depends on how beer is kept, you know. I should think they've got a good cellarman.'

'It's quite a nice place,' said Vicky. 'I like it.'

'The barmaid looks a bit supercilious,' said Gordon. 'Nasty-smell-under-the-nose-blonde.'

Mr. Budd chuckled.

'They're mostly like that these days, Mr. Cross. Now when I was workin' on a beat . . . '

'Remember my wife's here,' interrupted Gordon severely.

'Don't mind me, Mr. Budd,' said Vicky. 'I'm hardened to anything since I married Gordon.'

'Well, I like that . . . ' began Gordon indignantly.

'Being married to me, darling?' she asked sweetly.

'That wasn't what I meant,' he said.

'You should get out of the habit of using slang,' she retorted. 'Well, what did you think of Maurice Swayne, Mr. Budd?'

The big man took another long drink of beer before he replied. Then he said thoughtfully:

'Can't say I was very impressed, Mrs. Cross. Full o' hot air 'e seemed ter me. In spite o' that dramatic announcement of his 'e couldn't tell us much, could 'e?'

'Couldn't — or *didn't*?' said Gordon.

'H'm . . . maybe there's a lot in that,' agreed Mr. Budd. 'All he saw was somebody runnin' away from Lord Latimer's property. 'E couldn't say who it was or what they was like . . . Nuthin' 'elpful at all . . . '

'I wouldn't put any credance on what Swayne says,' said Gordon. 'I don't believe he came just to tell us what he saw . . . '

'Then what *did* 'e come for?' demanded Mr. Budd.

'I don't know, but you can bet it was something to the advantage of Maurice Swayne,' answered Gordon. 'I've told you what sort of a man he is.'

'A really nasty piece of work,' put in Vicky.

'I'm 'avin' 'im checked up,' said Mr. Budd. 'Didn't it strike you as queer he should know Kenwood?'

'There's a lot that's queer about Maurice Swayne,' said Gordon.

'Why,' interposed Vicky, 'did he pick out that tune on the piano?'

'Yes,' said Gordon, nodding, 'yes, *why* did he?'

'Because 'e 'eard somebody whistlin' it — the man who ran away,' said Mr.

Budd, 'an' it stuck in 'is mind. That's what 'e said . . . '

'Yes, that's what he *said*,' replied Gordon, 'but I don't think it was the *real* answer. Mr. Swayne's line of business is blackmail . . . '

'Do you mean he was using a subtle method of letting somebody know that he knew something?' asked Vicky.

'Or to see what effect the playing of that tune would have on — somebody,' said Gordon Cross quietly.

Mr. Budd picked up his tankard and swirled the remaining contents gently.

'Well, you don't have to look very far to know who, if that was it,' he murmured softly. 'You know 'ow it affected a certain party, Mrs. Cross?'

Vicky nodded her dark head.

'Yes, I did,' she said. 'David Kenwood . . . Gordon, did you see his face?'

'No,' answered Gordon. 'No, I wasn't looking at *his* face.'

Vicky gave him a quick glance.

'Whose face were you looking at?' she demanded.

There was an appreciable silence before

he replied. Then he said, speaking very slowly and deliberately:

'Iris Latimer's.'

III

Six days passed slowly by. The heat wave showed no sign of breaking. Indeed the temperature rose steadily until it constituted a record. The whole country lay sizzling under a sun that blazed down with almost tropical intensity. Mr. Budd, perplexed and perspiring, went ponderously about his business and put in a great deal of work without any tangible result to show for his efforts.

The man who called himself the Tipster had shot Lord Latimer and apparently vanished from the face of the earth. The *Daily Clarion* had received no other call and the bored but patient men who took it in turns to listen in on the telephone line heard nothing to reward them for their diligence.

Gordon Cross waited as day after day went by with increasing impatience. The sensational beginning had not borne the fruit he had hoped for and expected.

Vicky looked across at him as he lay on the settee in the sitting-room of their small flat in Bloomsbury, his eyes fixed on the ceiling.

'Have you got a cigarette, darling?' she asked. There was no reply, and she tried again slightly louder. 'Gordon, will you give me a cigarette?'

Still no answer.

'Gordon Cross,' she cried, 'I'm asking you for a cigarette . . . '

He sat up with a jerk.

'Eh?' he said. 'What . . . Cigarette? You'll find a packet in my pocket . . . hanging on that chair. Give me one, too, will you? And the matches.'

'Why don't you get up and get them yourself?' she demanded.

'I'm thinking . . . '

She uttered a derisive sound.

'That's a beautiful excuse for being lazy,' she said. 'Do you know it's exactly a week to-night since Lord Latimer was murdered and you've done absolutely nothing . . . Gordon Cross plastered across the front page of the *Clarion* — huh! In the obituary column with 'dead from the neck up' is more like it . . . '

'That is definitely rude,' said Gordon.

'Well,' she said impatiently, 'why don't you *do* something . . . '

'I'm waiting for the Tipster to make his second move,' he replied.

'Supposing he doesn't?' demanded Vicky. 'What then? Are you going to spend the rest of your life lying about the place — waiting?'

'He will,' said Gordon confidently. 'If he doesn't then I'm wrong about the whole thing . . . '

'*That* wouldn't surprise me a whole lot,' she remarked.

'He's *got* to.' He got up from the settee and went over to his jacket on the back of the chair, and took from the pocket a packet of cigarettes. He gave one to Vicky and took one himself.

'He's got to, Vicky. If he just dries up after the Latimer affair, there isn't the big story I think there is.'

'I suppose it hasn't occurred to your rapidly declining intellect, darling,' said

Vicky sarcastically, 'that somebody just wanted to kill Latimer and used all that stuff about the Tipster, and ringing up the *Clarion*, and the four other people, as a blind . . . ?'

'Of course it has, but I don't believe it . . . '

'That's pure wishful thinking,' she said.

'Maybe it is, but I don't think so, Vicky.' He drew quickly on the cigarette and blew out a cloud of smoke. 'There's something more at the back of it . . . '

'Well, he's dried up since Latimer was murdered,' said Vicky. 'That doesn't look too promising for your theory.'

'He's probably planning the next,' said Gordon.

'If there's to be a next,' she remarked. 'You know darling, you're rather determined to treat this like a thriller story. You even tried to drag Iris Latimer in as a suspect . . . '

'I'm jolly sure she knows something about it,' declared Gordon. 'Something she hasn't told the police. If you'd been looking at her instead of at Kenwood, that day when Swayne arrived, you'd agree.

She suddenly thought of something — and it horrified her.'

'You are not suggesting,' said Vicky, 'that she's in league with the Tipster, are you?'

He frowned. He said, shaking his head:

'No . . . no, but I believe, at the moment when I caught that expression on her face, she had a suspicion who he might be.'

'Then why didn't she tell the police?'

'I don't know . . . '

'Who could it be, Gordon?' said Vicky thoughtfully. 'The police have checked up on Kenwood and Swayne, and either of them could have put through that call to the *Clarion* and shot Lord Latimer. But there's no motive. Mr. Budd took the trouble to verify Masters's statement that he went to the pictures and called in at the *Compasses* afterwards for a drink. The girl in the box-office remembers him and so does the barmaid. Anyway, what motive could *he* have had?'

Gordon nodded.

'It all comes back to that, darling,' he said, 'the motive. If we could only find out what *that* is, the rest would be easy . . . '

'Unless the Tipster's a lunatic,' said Vicky. 'There doesn't have to be a motive then, and there's no reason why he should ever turn up again . . . '

The clock on the mantelpiece softly chimed nine and Gordon looked over at it.

'It was this time last Thursday that the Tipster . . . ' he began and was interrupted by the sudden ringing of the telephone bell. Vicky, startled at the coincidence, stood with her mouth slightly open and her large eyes round with surprise as he went over to the instrument and picked up the receiver.

'Hello,' he called, 'Gordon Cross here . . . '

Mr. Budd's voice broke in rapidly.

'The *Clarion* 'ad another call from the Tipster just before nine,' he said, 'our man was listenin' in . . . It was a Toll call this time — public call-box in Epsom district . . . '

'Who is the victim this time?' broke in Gordon.

46

'Man called Crawford,' answered Mr. Budd. 'James Crawford — trainer of race 'orses — lives at Epsom. We're goin' there now . . . pick you up in the police car outside your flat?'

'Right, I'll be there,' Gordon banged the receiver down on its rest and turned to Vicky, his face flushed with excitement.

'Get your things on, darling,' he said. 'We're going to Epsom. I *was* right. The Tipster's made his second move.'

IV

'I've telephoned the Epsom p'lice,' said Mr. Budd, as they sped along in the police car. 'They're goin' straight away to this feller Crawford's 'ouse an' wait for us . . . '

'Did you warn Crawford?' asked Gordon Cross, quickly.

'Tried to,' said the big man, 'but 'is line was dead — couldn't get through . . . '

'I'll bet the Tipster cut it before he phoned the *Clarion*,' said Gordon. 'He'd guess that's what you'd try and do . . . '

''E won't get away with it *this* time,' declared Mr. Budd, confidently. 'The local p'lice'll get there before 'im . . . '

'Perhaps he *has* got away with it,' suggested Vicky. 'Supposing he killed Crawford *before* he telephoned the *Clarion*?'

'He wouldn't do *that*,' said Gordon, shaking his head. 'His *vanity* wouldn't let him. Can't you sense the colossal egoism behind his method? He tells you what he's going to do and *challenges* you to prevent it . . . '

'If you ask me 'e's a stark, starin' maniac,' grunted Mr. Budd.

'That's what *I* think,' said Vicky, 'but Gordon won't agree.'

'He's undoubtedly a paranoic,' said Gordon, 'but I don't think he's mad in the way *you* mean. There's a practical motive behind it all . . . '

'If there is,' said Vicky quickly, 'it's connected in some way with racing. It just couldn't be a coincidence that he calls himself the Tipster, that Lord Latimer was Senior Steward of the Jockey Club, and now this man, Crawford, a trainer of race horses . . . '

'I believe you've got something there, darling,' said Gordon.

'Of course I have,' she said. 'It's obvious . . . '

'Maybe Crawford'll be able to tell us somethin' about that,' remarked Mr. Budd hopefully.

Gordon Cross shrugged his shoulders.

'I doubt it,' he answered, 'even if he's still alive.'

The powerful police car, unhampered by such things as speed limits, made short work of the journey and presently they came in sight of a pair of large gates.

''Ere we are,' said Mr. Budd. 'This is the place . . . drive in through them gates . . . '

They swung into a cobbled courtyard and were almost instantly hailed by a constable who had apparently been waiting for them to arrive.

'You Sup'n'tendent Budd, sir?' he asked, as the big man got heavily out.

Mr. Budd nodded.

'I was told to expect you, sir,' the man continued. 'Inspector Rogers an' Sergeant

Day've gone to look for Mr. Crawford . . .'

'Isn't 'e at 'ome?' demanded Mr. Budd quickly.

'No, sir,' said the constable. 'He went out a few minutes before we got 'ere, sir . . .'

'Where'd he go? D'you know?' interposed Gordon sharply.

'No, sir,' said the constable.

'I don't like it, Budd.' Gordon turned a troubled face towards the stout detective. 'I'm afraid we're going to be too late.'

'Did Crawford go out alone?' asked Mr. Budd.

'Yes, sir.'

'What took 'im out — did 'e 'ave a telephone message or somethin'?'

'I don't know, sir,' answered the constable.

'Is there *anybody* in the house?'

'Only Mrs. Brockett, sir — the 'ouse-keeper,' said the constable. 'The head lad and stable boys live over the stables . . .'

'We'd better go an' see this woman,' grunted Mr. Budd. 'P'raps she'll be able to . . .'

'Look!' exclaimed Vicky suddenly. 'There's

somebody running across that field over there . . . '

She pointed and Gordon made out the figure of a man stumbling towards them and waving his arms.

'He's trying to attract our attention . . . '

'It's Sergeant Day,' said the constable.

'Come on, Budd,' said Gordon, starting to run towards the gate opening into the field. 'Let's go and meet him. I think he's found something . . . '

Mr. Budd lumbered heavily along in his wake, breathing stertorously and jerkily. Gordon reached the gate first and waited for the big man to come up with him. Sergeant Day was only a few yards away and Mr. Budd and he reached the gate almost together.

'You . . . from the Yard, sir?' panted the sergeant. 'Inspector Rogers . . . sent me . . . back to . . . see . . . if you'd arrived . . . '

'What is it, sergeant?' asked Mr. Budd breathlessly, and red in the face from his exertions.

'We've found Mr. Crawford, sir,' said

Sergeant Day with difficulty. 'Over . . . there in . . . the spinney . . . He's dead . . . '

'How . . . how was he killed?' broke in Gordon.

'Stabbed, sir,' said the sergeant, 'in the back.'

3

I

In the gloomy depths of the spinney they stood looking down at the man who lay face downwards and almost hidden by a mass of straggling bushes. On the back of his light tweed jacket a dull red stain was spreading slowly as the blood soaked into the cloth.

'It's horrible, Gordon — horrible,' breathed Vicky unsteadily.

'I told you to stay behind in the field,' he said.

'I . . . wanted to . . . to see . . . ' she whispered.

Mr. Budd stooped, touched the body gently and looked up.

''E's dead all right,' he murmured. 'Stabbed twice by the look of it. We'll 'ave ter get a doctor . . . '

'Cut along to that phone box and ring up the station, Day,' ordered Inspector Rogers. 'Tell 'em to get hold of the divisional surgeon at once an' send him along. You wait for him at the phone box and bring him here.'

'Right you are, sir,' said Sergeant Day briskly, and departed, to vanish almost at once among the thickly growing trees.

'There's no weapon,' said Mr. Budd, 'so I s'pose the murderer took it with 'im . . . 'Ave you searched the body?'

Inspector Rogers nodded.

'Yes,' he answered. 'I found this note in his jacket pocket.'

He produced a folded slip of paper which he handed to the big man, handling it carefully in gloved hands.

Mr. Budd took it gingerly, unfolded it and scrutinized it through half-closed eyes.

'H'm!' he remarked. ''I'll be in the wood behind the house at 9.15. We can talk without bein' over-'eard. I shan't wait, so be on time.' Typewritten, no signature. Did you find any envelope?'

'No, sir,' said the inspector.

'Well, that accounts for Crawford's bein' here,' commented Mr. Budd. 'I wonder who 'e *thought* that note was from?' He folded the paper and put it in his wallet.

' 'Ow far away is this call-box — the one the Tipster made 'is call from?'

'It's on the road, sir,' said Rogers. 'Not five minutes away if you take the short cut by the footpath . . . '

' 'E rang up the *Clarion* just before nine,' murmured Mr. Budd, gently stroking his cascade of chins. 'H'm, 'e'd 'ave had plenty of time . . . '

'It was just before nine the first time, wasn't it?' said Gordon.

Mr. Budd nodded slowly.

'Yes . . . I wonder if there's anythin' in that — the time? I think I'll go an' find that call-box, Mr. Cross. There's a couple of calls I'd like ter make meself. I'd like ter know if those fellers Swayne and Kenwood are at 'ome this evenin' . . . '

'Listen!' interrupted Vicky suddenly. They listened. Mingling with the twittering of the birds which had formed a ceaseless background, came another sound — the faint sound of some whistling . . .

'Can you hear it?' whispered Vicky.

'Yes . . . be quiet,' muttered Gordon. 'There's somebody coming . . . through those trees . . . '

The faint whistling grew louder — the unmistakable melody of 'Clair de Lune' — and they watched in breathless silence staring at the little glade from which the sound came. Presently a figure came in sight — a man's figure walking slowly towards them. The bushes hid their presence and it wasn't until he was almost on them that he saw them. The whistling stopped abruptly.

'Good evening, Mr. Swayne,' said Gordon Cross, pleasantly. 'What are you doing here?'

Maurice Swayne stared at him and then at the sprawling figure of Crawford.

'What's happened?' he demanded, huskily. 'Who . . . who's that?'

'It *was* a gentleman called James Crawford,' replied Gordon.

'*Was?*' Swayne licked his lips. 'Has there been an accident? Is he — dead?'

'He's dead, but it wasn't an accident,' said Gordon. 'The Tipster has been a very busy man this evening . . . '

'The Tipster?' Swayne looked quickly from one to the other. 'You don't mean . . . this is another — murder?'

'It's murder right enough,' said Mr. Budd curtly. 'An' I should like you to explain 'ow you come to be in the vicinity so soon after the crime was committed.'

Uneasiness flickered for a moment in the man's eyes. Then he recovered himself. He said, with all his old blandness:

'Merely an unfortunate coincidence, Superintendent, I assure you.'

'You didn't see the murderer *this* time, then Mr. Swayne?' said Gordon sarcastically.

For a second the blandness wavered.

'I . . . I don't understand,' said Maurice Swayne uneasily.

'It was a coincidence that you happened to be near Lord Latimer's house at the time *he* was murdered, wasn't it?' said Gordon.

'Yes, of course. I've already explained that . . . '

'And now by another — er — coincidence,' Gordon went on, 'you happen to be here just after Crawford is murdered. Two murders and two coincidences . . . I should be careful not to let these coincidences happen too frequently, Mr.

Swayne. You know, it's apt to give people a wrong impression.'

II

It was late when Gordon and Vicky got back to their flat. Mr. Budd had shown a great display of energy. He had questioned the housekeeper, Mrs. Brockett, who turned out to be almost stone deaf and of no practical help at all. She couldn't say how the note had come into James Crawford's possession, or exactly when he had gone out. She had gone upstairs for a few minutes and when she came down, he was gone.

Mr. Maurice Swayne was equally unhelpful. He produced a perfect alibi for the time of the murder and all inquiries failed to shake it.

They said good night to a rather disgruntled Mr. Budd and let themselves into the flat.

'I think they should have arrested Swayne,' declared Vicky, stripping off her light summer coat and flinging it over the back of a chair.

'They couldn't have held him,' said Gordon, 'there wasn't enough evidence . . . '

'He was *there*, wasn't he?' she demanded. '*And* he was whistling that tune . . . '

'You can't arrest a man for walking in the country and whistling a tune, darling . . . '

'Well, it's a jolly queer coincidence . . . '

'I agree with you,' he said, a little absently. 'In fact, I don't think it was a coincidence.'

'Then *you* think Swayne is the Tipster?' she said, quickly.

'I didn't say so.' He lit a cigarette and dropped into a chair. 'But I don't believe his explanation — that he'd been on a visit to some friends and was taking a short cut to the station — although they confirmed his statement . . . '

'An Armenian half-caste and his wife — if she *was* his wife,' said Vicky scornfully.

'He wasn't an Armenian,' grunted Gordon.

'Well, whatever he was, I should think he'd say anything — and so would she.'

'Quite probably. But what they did say was enough to stop Swayne being arrested . . . '

'I don't care what you say . . . ' she came over and perched on the arm of his chair . . . 'it's queer. Latimer's murdered and Swayne turns up *there*. Crawford's murdered and Swayne turns up *there*, too . . . '

'I'm willing to admit it's queer,' said Gordon, 'I let Swayne know I thought so, too. But it doesn't necessarily mean that he's the Tipster. I don't think he's the right type. I can't imagine Swayne committing murder unless he was driven into a tight corner and couldn't get out by any other means . . . '

'Perhaps that's what's happened?' said Vicky. She ran her fingers lightly through his hair.

'Even then he wouldn't go in for all those fancy trimmings,' said Gordon. 'There's a different type of mind at work there — a queer, distorted sort of mind — with an urge to dramatize itself . . . '

'Well, he's taking appalling risks to satisfy it,' she said.

'I think that's what makes it all the more worth while,' he said. 'He's *got* to show how clever he is — it's a sort of kink. That's the reason for the telephone calls to the *Clarion* and the choice of his alias . . . '

'Whatever you think about it, it sounds mad to me,' said Vicky.

'Oh, he's definitely unbalanced. There's no doubt about that. All I'm maintaining is that there's a logical reason for these killings . . . ' He got up and went over to the lamp. 'What do you make of this, darling?'

She followed him quickly. He was examining something under the light.

'What is it?' she began, and as she saw what it was he was holding: 'Gordon, where did you get *that*?'

'Didn't you see me pick it up? It was lying under that bush. I knew the others didn't see me but I thought you did. It was just before Swayne put in his appearance . . . '

'It's a handkerchief,' she said, staring at it . . . 'all over blood . . . '

'Yes.' He turned the ugly-looking thing delicately over with one finger. 'It was used to wipe the knife that killed Crawford.'

Vicky gave a little shiver. She said disgustedly:

'Ugh! How beastly . . . '

'D'you notice anything — particular — about it?' he asked.

'It's a *woman's* handkerchief . . . '

'Yes, but I didn't mean that.' He held it out closer to her. 'Smell it,' he said.

She forced herself not to back away, and sniffed.

'Gordon,' she exclaimed, 'that's the perfume Iris Latimer uses . . . '

He nodded.

'Yes,' he answered. 'Yes, I rather thought it was. I think we ought to pay her a visit in the morning, don't you? It might be interesting to discover how one of Iris Latimer's handkerchiefs came into possession of the Tipster?'

III

The morning was the hottest of that long spell of tropical weather. Gordon Cross wiped his damp face before he raised his hand to knock at the front door of White Gables.

'If it gets any hotter I shall melt,' he said. 'Phew! It's a scorcher this morning . . . '

'Oh, do stop grumbling, Gordon,' said Vicky. 'It's lovely . . . '

'*You're* all right,' he said, eyeing the lightly-clad figure of his wife. 'You've scarcely got anything on . . . '

The door opened before she could reply and Masters looked at them inquiringly. It was obvious that he did not remember them.

'Good morning, Masters,' said Gordon. 'Is Miss Latimer at home?'

'Who shall I say it is, sir?' asked the butler uncertainly.

'Cross — Gordon Cross. I was here last week with Superintendent Budd.'

Masters' face cleared.

'I remember you now, sir,' he said. 'I beg your pardon. Will you come in, please? I will inquire if Miss Latimer will see you.'

He stood, aside and they entered the cool house.

'What are you going to say to her?' whispered Vicky, as the butler left them.

'It depends. I shall use my own discretion,' said Gordon.

'That's what I was afraid of,' she answered.

They hadn't long to wait. Masters came

back and informed them that his mistress was in the drawing-room and would see them. He led the way and ushered them into the long, pleasantly cool room.

'Good morning, Miss Latimer,' said Gordon. 'I'm sorry to disturb you but the matter is rather important. This is my wife . . . '

'How do you do,' said Iris. 'Do sit down, won't you?'

'Thank you,' said Vicky. She thought the girl looked pale and wan — as though she hadn't slept very well.

'It's a lovely morning, isn't it?' said Iris, politely.

'My husband doesn't think so,' answered Vicky. 'He's been grumbling about the heat ever since we left London . . . '

'Don't you like this weather, Mr. Cross?' asked Iris.

'Not as hot as this,' he answered.

'I love it. It can't be too hot for me,' she said.

'Or me,' said Vicky.

'What did you wish to see me about, Mr. Cross?' said Iris. 'You were with the police, weren't you? I didn't know who you were until Masters explained . . . '

'I'm afraid we weren't introduced on that occasion,' said Gordon.

'Have you come to give me any news,' asked Iris, eagerly. 'Have they found the man who . . . '

'Not yet, I'm afraid, Miss Latimer . . . '

'Oh . . . ' She was obviously disappointed. 'Then what have you . . . '

'Have you seen the *Clarion* this morning, Miss Latimer?' asked Gordon.

She shook her head.

'No, we don't have the *Clarion*, Mr. Cross . . . '

'Pity,' he said. 'There's been another Tipster murder, Miss Latimer. The other newspapers haven't got the story yet . . . '

'*Another?*' Her face went even paler than it had been before. 'Who . . . who was it?'

'A man called James Crawford,' said Gordon, slowly. 'The Tipster killed him last night — after telephoning his intention to the *Clarion*.'

'James Crawford,' she said, quickly, 'the *trainer?*'

'You — knew him?'

65

'I never met him — I knew of him, of course,' she answered. 'He hasn't — hadn't, I suppose I should say — a very good reputation. Mr. Cross . . . ' she leaned forward. 'Why don't the police do something about this man? If they knew he was going to — to kill Mr. Crawford, surely they could have stopped him . . . ?'

'They did their best,' said Gordon. 'Crawford was found dead in a little wood near his home . . . '

'How dreadful,' said Iris.

'Perhaps you know the place, Miss Latimer?'

'No, no, I don't . . . '

'You've never been to Crawford's training stables?'

'No, never,' she said. 'My father knew him. I didn't. He didn't like him very much. He always said that Crawford was a crook. On two occasions he narrowly escaped being 'warned off' . . . Why did this man — the Tipster — kill him?'

'There doesn't appear to be any reason, Miss Latimer . . . '

'I'm sure he must be insane,' she declared. 'There can't be any other explanation . . . '

'At any rate,' he remarked, 'that seems to be the most popular one.'

She looked at him quickly.

'Does that mean — *you* don't think so?'

'To be quite candid, I don't,' he said. 'You must understand, though, that it is only my own personal opinion. I have no evidence to justify it . . . '

'But you must have some reason for thinking it?'

'I should call it a hunch,' he said, and then in a different tone: 'Were you at home yesterday evening?'

She stared in surprise at the sudden question.

'Why?' she asked.

'*Were* you?' he repeated.

'Well, no, I wasn't,' she answered. 'I went to London on business. Why are you asking these questions, Mr. Cross?'

'Crawford was stabbed to death,' said Gordon. 'The murderer took the knife away with him. But he wiped it first — on *this* . . . '

He took the bloodstained handkerchief

from his pocket and held it out to her. She gave a little exclamation of disgust.

'Look at it, Miss Latimer . . . '

'I don't want to,' she cried. 'It's horrible . . . '

'The perfume you use . . . It's called 'Sans Adieu,' isn't it?' asked Vicky.

'Yes, but . . . '

'That is a woman's handkerchief,' said Vicky, 'and it smells of 'Sans Adieu.''

'Oh!' Iris's eyes widened with horror. 'I . . . '

There came the sudden sound of voices outside the door. They heard Masters say: 'I'll tell Miss Iris you're here, Miss Kenwood.'

A woman's voice, a deep contralto, said: 'Don't bother, Masters. We'll announce ourselves . . . '

The door was opened quickly and a tall, beautifully dressed woman came in, followed by David Kenwood.

'Hullo, Iris,' she said. 'We're on our way up to town and we thought we'd pop in and see if . . . why, what's the matter?'

Iris turned towards her with obvious relief.

'Lydia — David — I'm so glad you've come . . . I . . . '

'What's happened, Iris?' asked Kenwood anxiously.

'There was another murder last night, David,' she said. 'The Tipster killed James Crawford, the trainer . . . '

'The Tipster?' he interrupted.

She nodded.

'I don't see why you should be so upset, Iris,' remarked Lydia Kenwood. 'You didn't know this man, Crawford, did you?'

'It isn't that . . . '

'Then what's the trouble?' demanded Kenwood.

'They found a handkerchief — a woman's handkerchief . . . ' Iris was tearful and slightly incoherent . . . 'all over blood . . . with my perfume on it . . . '

'*Yours?*' interjected Kenwood. 'But you don't often use any . . . '

'This was a present . . . from Lydia . . . ' said Iris. 'Don't you remember, David? You brought over three bottles of 'Sans Adieu' for her from Paris last Christmas and she gave me one . . . '

69

'*I* remember,' said Lydia.

'Do *you* use 'Sans Adieu,' Miss Kenwood?' asked Gordon Cross.

'Yes, always,' she nodded. 'It's my favourite perfume . . . '

'Then this handkerchief could equally well belong to either of you?' said Gordon.

Lydia Kenwood looked at him calmly. Her large grey eyes were cold.

'Or to neither of us,' she retorted coolly. 'Miss Latimer and I are not the *only* users of 'Sans Adieu' in the world, you know . . . '

'No,' he replied, quickly, 'but you are the only two people who use it, so far as we know, who are mixed up in this business.'

'And it's not very easily obtainable these days, is it?' put in Vicky.

'Are you suggesting,' snapped Kenwood angrily, 'that Miss Latimer, or my sister, has something to do with the murder of Crawford?'

'I'm not suggesting anything,' said Gordon, quietly. 'This handkerchief was found near the body. It was used to wipe the knife that killed this man. I'm only interested to know how it got there . . . '

'It must have been dropped by the Tipster . . . '

'Exactly.'

'You surely don't imagine,' said Lydia, in a voice that was completely hostile, 'that Iris, or I, is the Tipster, Mr. — er — er . . . '

'Cross. I merely want to know how this could have come into the Tipster's possession, Miss Kenwood . . . '

'I'm afraid we really couldn't tell you,' she sneered. 'You'd better catch him and find out . . . '

'I intend to,' he said, easily.

'Surely,' said Kenwood, a little more calmly, 'it could be anybody's handkerchief? Why are you certain it belongs to Iris Latimer?'

'It doesn't, David,' interrupted his sister. 'It's one of mine.'

'Yours?' he exclaimed, completely taken aback.

'Yes,' she said. 'I had a dozen of them. Quite a lot have got lost one way or another . . . '

'Why didn't you say this was yours in the first place, Miss Kenwood?' demanded Gordon.

'Why should I?' she asked. 'I don't recognize your right to question me, Mr. — er — Cross . . . '

'I'm sorry you should adopt that attitude,' said Gordon. 'Perhaps you would prefer the police?'

David Kenwood tried to pour a little oil on the troubled waters.

'I don't see why you should get huffy, Lydia,' he said. 'Cross is only trying to find out the truth. That's what we all want to do, isn't it? You must admit it's damned queer how that handkerchief came to be found where it did. Are you *sure* it's one of yours?'

'Quite sure,' she answered.

'Then how could this man have got hold of it?'

'I've told you I've lost several of them at odd times,' she said wearily. 'Beyond that, I haven't the least idea.' She looked at the jewelled watch on her wrist.

'Don't you think we ought to be going?'

'Yes, I suppose we ought.' He sounded a trifle reluctant. 'Are you coming, Iris?'

Iris shook her head.

'No, I don't think I will, David,' she said. 'I've a lot of letters to write and . . . '

There was a tap on the door and Masters came in.

'Mr. Maurice Swayne is here, miss,' he announced. 'Shall I . . . ?'

But before he could complete the sentence Maurice Swayne had pushed round him and was in the room.

'Well, well, quite a gathering,' he greeted, smoothly, his small eyes passing rapidly from one to the other. 'Mr. Cross — and Mrs. Cross, too . . . How delightful to see you both again so soon. *So* sorry to intrude, Miss Latimer, but I was on my way to see Kenwood, and recognized his car in your drive . . . '

'I told you I was going out this morning,' broke in David Kenwood crossly. He looked thoroughly annoyed but Mr. Swayne was impervious to bad temper.

'Yes . . . Isn't it lucky I managed to catch you in time?' he said blandly. 'I wonder if you're going to town, whether you'd give me a lift? Have you caught that fellow — what's-his-name — the Tipster — yet, Mr. Cross?'

'No — not yet,' said Gordon.

'I wonder if you will?' Mr. Swayne pursed his lips. 'It's my opinion he'll prove too clever for you all . . . '

'What makes you think that, Mr. Swayne?' asked Gordon. 'Inside information?'

IV

'Well,' remarked Vicky, as they sped along the winding country road on the way back to London, '*that* didn't get us much further, did it, darling?'

'Eh?' asked Gordon absently.

'I said that didn't get us much further, did it?' she repeated.

'Sorry, Vicky, I didn't hear you,' he said. 'I was thinking . . . '

'Go on,' she said. 'Don't let me stop you . . . '

'At least we know to whom that

handkerchief belonged,' he said.

'If Lydia Kenwood was telling the truth,' she commented.

'She'd hardly admit it was hers if it wasn't . . . '

'Oh, I don't know,' said Vicky. 'I can imagine certain circumstances in which she might . . . '

'Such as?' asked Gordon.

'Well, if she wanted to shield somebody for instance . . . '

'H'm . . . perhaps . . . who do you think it might be?'

'Obviously the most likely person would be her brother,' she said.

'Yes . . . or Maurice Swayne,' he suggested.

Vicky looked round at him in surprise.

'I don't see why,' she said.

He swung the car round a sharp bend before replying.

'We don't know what the relationship is between the Kenwoods and Swayne, do we?'

'No . . . but I don't think there's much love lost between them,' she said. 'Gordon, *do* be careful what you're doing. We nearly swerved into that ditch . . . '

'Sorry, darling,' he apologized, frowning. 'I don't quite know what happened . . . we must have skidded on a loose stone or something . . . '

'Well, be more careful . . . You shouldn't drive so fast . . . '

'Fast?' He laughed. 'You *couldn't* drive fast with this car . . . '

'What were you saying about the Kenwoods?'

'I don't think there's much love lost between the Kenwoods and Maurice Swayne.'

'Not outwardly, I agree,' he said. 'But I wonder if we can judge by outward appearances . . . '

The car wobbled dangerously and Vicky gave a cry of alarm.

'Gordon, what is the matter with you?' she demanded. 'You're all over the road . . . '

'I don't know,' he confessed, with a puzzled frown.

'Well, you'd better pull yourself together . . . there's a sharp bend just ahead of us

. . . Gordon, look out! You're going straight for that brick wall . . . '

'I can't help it,' he cried, wrenching at the wheel.

'Gordon!'

'Something's wrong with the steering . . . ' he said. 'Jump, Vicky . . . open the door and jump . . . '

His foot came down hard on the clutch pedal and at the same time he jammed on the brakes. But it was too late. The car lurched and skidded and with the brake drums screaming in protest crashed into the low brick wall that guarded one side of the hairpin bend. There was a jangle of breaking glass, the car bounced back from the impact and turned over, flinging Vicky and Gordon together in a heap and knocking the breath out of them.

4

I

Vicky was the first to recover from the shock of the smash.

'Gordon . . . ' she whispered shakily. 'Gordon . . . '

'Are you all right . . . Vicky?' he asked.

'I . . . don't know,' she answered. 'I . . . can't move . . . '

'Are you . . . hurt?'

'I don't think so . . . I feel a bit . . . bruised . . . '

'Keep still,' said Gordon. 'I'm going to try and get this door open . . . '

He shifted his position gingerly. The door was above him and wedging his foot on the seat he twisted the handle and pushed. It wouldn't budge.

'It must have jammed when the car turned over . . . ' he said breathlessly. He tried again and felt it give a little. 'I think it's coming,' he said, and put forth all his remaining strength. The door came free and he flung it back.

'That's got it,' he gasped. 'Just a minute, darling, and I'll get you out . . . '

He hauled himself up and scrambled out.

'Now,' he said, leaning through the open door and looking down at his wife, 'give me your hand . . . '

'Be careful,' she said, 'I'm wedged in . . . '

He gave her arm a gentle tug.

'Oh!' she cried.

'Sorry, Vicky,' he said, relaxing his grip.

'It's all right, darling.' She wriggled round into a different position.

'Catch hold of the wheel with your other hand,' he said. 'That's right . . . now put your foot on the seat . . . '

'I'm slipping . . . ' she said.

'You won't slip . . . I've got you,' said Gordon. 'Now, up you come . . . '

He pulled her up, and presently she was sitting, breathless and dishevelled beside him on the top of the overturned car.

'All right?' he asked.

'Yes, I think so,' she answered. 'I feel a bit sore and shaken . . . Gordon, what happened?'

'Something went wrong with the steering . . . If I hadn't braked hard there would have been a worse crash . . . '

'This was bad enough,' she said. 'What could have gone wrong?'

He shook his head.

'I don't know,' he said. 'I'm going to have a look . . . '

He slid down into the roadway and went round to the front of the car. After a moment or two she heard him utter a low whistle.

'Here's the trouble, darling,' he called. 'One of the front wheels came off . . . '

'Gordon!' she gasped. 'We might have been killed . . . '

'Yes,' he answered gravely. 'Yes . . . I think that was the intention . . . '

'Intention?' She suddenly grasped his meaning. 'You mean . . . it wasn't an accident?'

'Yes. Come here, Vicky . . . '

She got gingerly down into the roadway and limped towards him.

'Look at these bolts,' said Gordon. 'Do you see all those fresh scratches?'

'Yes . . . '

'They weren't there when we started from London this morning. They were made by a spanner, darling . . . '

'But who could have?'

'We left the car in the drive while we interviewed Iris Latimer,' said Gordon. 'Anybody could have loosened these bolts. It wouldn't take very long . . . '

'Who do you think did it?' said Vicky, seriously.

He shook his head.

'I've no idea,' he said.

'Maurice Swayne might have done it, Gordon,' she said thoughtfully.

He rubbed his bruised arm and nodded thoughtfully.

'He might . . . The ubiquitous Mr. Swayne — he always seems to be around when there's any trouble, doesn't he?'

II

'That was quite a good lunch, darling,' said Vicky, leaning back in her chair contentedly. 'I feel much better . . . '

'Not bad, was it?' said Gordon. He held

out his cigarette-case and she took one.

They had left the wrecked car and walked to the nearest village where they had found a small café and succeeded in getting an excellent lunch. The little restaurant was almost next door to the railway station and Gordon had discovered there was a train at half-past one which would take them back to London.

'You know it's going to be awfully awkward, Gordon,' said Vicky, blowing a cloud of smoke towards the ceiling, 'without a car . . . '

'We may not have to do without one,' he answered. 'I telephoned the garage while I was at the station. I think they are going to lend us a car while ours is being repaired. There's not a great deal of serious damage . . . '

'I hope they do,' she said. 'You know, it's a lucky thing for us that wheel came off where it did. If it had happened in a busy street . . . '

'You're right,' he agreed. 'It wouldn't have been too good. Somebody's going to be disappointed about that . . . '

'Do you think it *could* have been Swayne?'

'It could have been anyone, darling,' he replied. 'Swayne, Kenwood, Masters . . . '

'*Masters?*' she repeated, incredulously.

'He had the same opportunity as the others . . . '

'But Masters *can't* be the Tipster . . . '

'Anybody could be the Tipster, Vicky,' he said. 'And it doesn't necessarily have to be anyone *we know* either . . . '

'No, I suppose not.' She nodded. 'It would have been a bit risky for a stranger, wouldn't it?'

'Not much more so than for anybody else,' said Gordon. 'We left the car close to that belt of shrubbery in the drive. The wheel that was tampered with was on the 'off side' — nearest the bushes — they'd have screened anyone's movements . . . '

She was silent for several seconds. Then she said suddenly:

'Why should the Tipster want to kill *us*?'

He laughed.

'Well, I take that as rather a compliment,' he said. 'Obviously he thinks we might be — dangerous . . . ' He looked at his watch. 'We'd better be going, darling . . . '

They paid the bill and walked round the corner to the station. It was only a tiny place and there were few people on the platform. There was still a minute before the train was due and they strolled up and down in the sun.

'What time do we get to London?' asked Vicky.

'Just after two,' he answered. 'It's a through train. Why on earth it stops here at all is a secret known only to the railway company . . . We'll get a taxi back to the flat and then I'll go round to the garage and see them about this car they're lending me . . . '

'Are you going to tell the police about this morning, Gordon?' she asked.

He thought for a moment and then shook his head.

'No, I don't think so,' he said. 'We'll just let everyone think it was an accident . . . '

The train came in at that moment and they found an empty compartment.

'Open the windows, Gordon,' said Vicky, as she settled herself in a corner seat. 'It's terribly stuffy in here . . . '

He lowered both windows and the train

started. Looking across at his wife a few minutes later he saw that she had fallen asleep and she slept until the train drew in at the London terminus.

'Now,' said Gordon, as they hurried up the platform, 'let's hope we can grab a taxi . . . '

They were passing through the barrier when Vicky suddenly gripped his arm.

'Listen,' she said, urgently.

The faint sound of somebody whistling reached him above the noise of the crowd.

'Clair de Lune,' breathed Vicky.

Gordon looked round. The crowd was dense. It was impossible to pick out the whistler.

'It's stopped now,' said Vicky. 'It came from over there . . . Someone in that crowd of people.'

He nodded.

'Yes,' he said. 'But — *who?*'

III

Mr. Budd came back from his lunch at the little tea-shop near Scotland Yard, which he invariably patronized and discovered that Colonel Blair, the Assistant Commissioner, wanted him in his office immediately.

With a sinking heart, for he guessed what the summons portended he made his way downstairs, and knocked at the Assistant Commissioner's door.

'Come in,' said Colonel Blair's voice, curtly and the big man entered reluctantly.

'Oh, it's you, Superintendent,' greeted the Assistant Commissioner, and frowned. 'I sent for you about this Crawford business . . .'

'Yes, sir,' said Mr. Budd, and waited for the deluge. It came — ice-cold and each word as brittle as an icicle.

'While I am quite willing to admit,' said Colonel Blair, 'that this Tipster business is unprecedented, that does not excuse your handling of the matter. You had warning that this man, Crawford, was going to be killed, and you failed to prevent it . . .'

'I took all the precautions that were possible, sir,' said Mr. Budd.

'Possibly,' said Colonel Blair coldly. 'Results, however, are the only things that count. This man is dead and his murderer remains at large. It won't do . . . it won't do at all . . . '

He went on for nearly a quarter of an hour on these lines, and when Mr. Budd eventually left the office the redness of his face was not entirely due to the heat.

The sympathetic Leek was waiting for him when he reached his own office.

'Was the old man mad?' he asked, as Mr. Budd squeezed himself into his chair. 'What did 'e 'ave ter say?'

The big man took a cigar from his waistcoat pocket and sniffed at it.

' 'E wanted to know when we was goin' ter bury you,' he grunted.

Leek looked at him in surprise.

'Bury me?' he repeated. 'I ain't dead . . . '

'You've been dead for years, but you don't know it,' snarled Mr. Budd. 'Did you get on to Cross?'

'There was no reply from his number,' said the aggrieved Sergeant Leek.

'I wonder what 'e's up to?' murmured

Mr. Budd, frowning.

'Maybe he's out somewhere?' suggested Leek helpfully, and the big man glared at him. Before he could give voice to his feelings, luckily for the sergeant, the telephone bell rang.

Mr. Budd grabbed the receiver.

'Sup'n'tendent Budd here,' he grunted. 'Who's that?'

'Detective-constable Johnson, sir,' was the urgent reply. 'There's another message from the Tipster just come through to the *Clarion* . . . '

'Go on,' snapped Mr. Budd.

'He states the name of his third victim is 'Tich' Dukes, the jockey,' went on Johnson quickly. 'The call came from a public call-box . . . '

'Where?' demanded the big man.

'Newbury district, sir . . . '

'Right,' said Mr. Budd. 'Stick at your post . . . '

He slammed the receiver back on the rack, and rapidly explained to Leek the gist of the message.

'See if you can get 'old o' Cross,' he ended, as he picked up his hat and lumbered to the door.

'Where are you goin'?' asked the sergeant.

'I'm goin' to find 'Tich' Dukes — before the Tipster does,' said Mr. Budd, and left the office.

An inquiry elicited the fact that 'Tich' Dukes was to be found at Hurst Park race-course and a fast police car sped him to the crowded course. He found 'Tich' Dukes in the saddling enclosure and explained the object of his visit.

The jockey, a wizened little man, with a sharp face, wrinkled like a walnut, was perturbed.

'You say this feller says he's going to kill *me*' he demanded in alarm.

'That's what 'e threatens ter do, but you needn't worry,' said Mr. Budd, soothingly. 'We'll see you don't come to any harm . . . '

'Tich' Dukes was not reassured.

'That's all very well,' he complained, 'what about Lord Latimer an' Crawford? You didn't stop *them* comin' to 'arm, did yer?'

'This is a different matter,' said the big

man. 'I'm takin' every precaution in your case. From now on you won't be left unguarded for an instant. Two detectives have been detailed to keep you under close observation. They'll remain with you all the time. You're in no danger at all . . . '

'I'm not so sure o' that,' said the jockey, looking uneasily about him. 'What about 'ere — all this crowd . . . 'E may be among 'em . . . '

'Maybe 'e is,' said Mr. Budd. 'But 'e won't 'ave an opportunity of gettin' at *you*. Make yer mind easy . . . '

'Easy?' echoed Dukes. 'It's all very well for you. This feller's insane — crazy — 'e might do anything . . . '

'Can you suggest any reason why he should want to kill you?' asked Mr. Budd, hopefully, but the jockey only shook his head.

'Reason?' he answered impatiently. 'What's the good of talkin' about reason when you're dealing with a lunatic? Of course 'e 'asn't got any reason . . . '

'We're not entirely satisfied that we are dealin' with a lunatic,' explained Mr.

Budd. 'There may be a motive behind these murders . . . '

'Tich' Dukes uttered a scornful sound.

'Was there a motive for Latimer an' Crawford?' he demanded.

'That's what we're tryin' to find out,' said Mr. Budd, and turned as a voice hailed him.

'Hello, Budd. Here you are, then . . . '

Gordon Cross and Vicky were coming towards him across the smooth turf.

'Hello, Mr. Cross,' said Mr. Budd. ''Ow are you, Mrs. Cross? Leek give you my message?'

'Yes, a few seconds after you left the Yard,' said Gordon. 'We must have been close behind you all the way. Leek came with us. He's over by the stands somewhere. The Tipster hasn't wasted much time, has he? Where'd the call come from?'

'Newbury — call-box,' said Mr. Budd.

'Newbury?' exclaimed Vicky. 'Gordon — did you hear that?'

He nodded.

'Curious, isn't it?' he said. 'I suppose you tried to catch him at the call-box?'

'Of course,' said the big man. 'The Newbury police was phoned while 'e was still talkin' to the *Clarion*, but by the time they'd found which call-box and rushed a man there, e'd gone . . . '

'There's not much chance of catching him *that* way,' said Gordon. 'I . . . '

'Look 'ere,' broke in 'Tich' Dukes. 'I'm ridin' in the next race and it's gettin' near the 'off.' I'll have to go an' get 'weighed out' . . . '

'My men'll go with you,' said Mr. Budd quickly. He beckoned to the two detectives he had brought with him. 'Don't let Mr. Dukes out of your sight, you two,' he ordered. 'Not for any consideration, you understand? I'm 'oldin' you responsible for 'is safety. I've fixed everythin' with the stewards so you can go anywhere without question . . . '

The trio moved off towards the weighing-room and Mr. Budd turned to Gordon Cross.

'Well, that's that,' he said, mopping his shiny face. 'I can't do any more except lock 'im up in a safe deposit . . . Where've you been all the morning, Mr. Cross?

Leek's tried to get you on the phone several times . . . '

'Tell you later,' said Gordon. 'Let's go up to the stand.'

They made their way out of the enclosure and through the throng of racegoers. The husky shouts of the bookmakers rose above the dull murmur of the crowd and Vicky turned towards her husband, her eyes bright and her cheeks flushed with excitement.

'Did you get a race-card?' she asked.

He gave her one and she studied it rapidly.

'Dukes is riding Summer Lightning,' he remarked.

She nodded.

'I like this one,' she said, after a pause. 'Inquisitive Lass . . . Put me ten bob each way on it, darling. They're offering a hundred-to-six.'

'What do you fancy, Budd?' asked Gordon.

'Well, a pint o' beer'ud go down nicely, Mr. Cross,' remarked the stout man. 'I seldom back 'orses — it's a mug's game . . . '

'Do you mean this doesn't thrill you, Mr. Budd?' said Vicky, in astonishment. 'I think racing is the most exciting thing in the world . . . '

'It's also the easiest way o' losin' money in the world, Mrs. Cross,' he retorted, and she laughed.

'You get a wonderful thrill while you're losing it,' she said.

'I'm going to have a quid on First Again,' said Gordon. 'Look after Vicky, will you, Budd?'

'Don't forget my ten bob each way on Inquisitive Lass,' Vicky called after him, and he nodded.

'I wonder if the Tipster *is* 'ere — somewhere among this crowd?' murmured Mr. Budd, as they walked slowly towards the stand. 'Hello — 'ere's my sergeant. Where've you been, eh? Gamblin' I'll be bound.'

'Well, I thought I might as well take a chance,' said Leek. 'A little extra money comes in 'andy now and again . . . '

'To the bookmakers, I s'pose you mean?' grunted Mr. Budd. ''Ow much of yer unearned income 'ave yer been squanderin' *this* time?'

'I 'aven't got any unearned income,' said the irate sergeant, 'all I've got is me pay . . . '

'That's what I meant,' said Mr. Budd scathingly.

'What did you back, Mr. Leek?' asked Vicky.

'A 'orse called Good-morning' answered the sergeant. 'I asked the bookmaker an' 'e said it was a good thin' . . . '

'Who for?' demanded Mr. Budd.

'It's forty-to-one,' said Leek. 'If it wins I shall get twenty quid . . . '

'An' if it don't the bookmaker gets ten bob,' said Mr. Budd. 'No wonder 'e told yer it was a good thin' . . . '

'The horses are down at the tapes,' said Gordon, joining them. 'The bell for the 'off' should go at any moment. Let's get a good position to see the race . . . '

They threaded their way through the mass of people on the stand and found a good place.

'Any second now,' said Gordon, and at that moment the bell sounded and a roar came up from the watching crowd. Away down the course little splashes of colour flashed in the sunshine and a sudden silence fell.

'I can't see very well, Gordon . . . ' said Vicky.

'Inquisitive Lass is still in the ruck,' said Gordon. 'There's a horse moving up . . . I think it's . . . yes, it's First Again . . . '

There was a sudden roar from the crowd. It swelled up over and around them. The horses were coming round the bend, a bunched mass with one a length ahead of the others.

'It's First Again's race,' cried Gordon excitedly. 'First Again'll win it . . . '

'What about Inquisitive Lass?' said Vicky, clutching his arm. 'Look at Inquisitive Lass, Gordon . . . Look . . . She's coming up, she's coming up . . . '

There were two horses now out in front of the rest, coming into the straight almost neck and neck. The excitement of the crowd was intense. There seemed little doubt that First Again or Inquisitive Lass would pass the post a winner. And then out from the bunch behind them came a brown streak . . .

'By Gosh!' shouted Gordon. 'Look at Summer Lightning . . . '

The brown horse swept forward, challenged and passed the two in front and flashed by the post . . .

'Summer Lightning's won it,' said Gordon.

'What's 'appened ter Good-mornin'?' asked Leek anxiously.

'They've changed it's name ter Good-night,' grunted Mr. Budd. 'You can say good-bye to that ten bob . . . '

'It was a great race,' said Gordon. 'Let's go along to the paddock.'

They mingled with the crowd that was pouring off the stand and as they made their way towards the paddock Vicky suddenly caught her husband's arm.

'Gordon — look over there,' she said. 'Surely that's Maurice Swayne?'

'Where?' asked Gordon, looking round.

'Over there,' she said, nodding towards the place.

'He's just turning in this direction . . . Oh, it's Masters . . . '

'It *can't* be Masters, darling,' said Gordon. 'How could he leave Newbury in the middle of the day?'

'It *is* Masters,' said Vicky. 'Look, he's seen us — he's coming this way . . . '

It was Masters. He came up to them and bowed a deferential greeting.

'Good afternoon, Mr. Cross,' he said. 'How do you do, Mrs. Cross?'

'Good afternoon, Masters,' said Vicky.

'Spending a day at the races?' asked Gordon.

The butler shook his head and smiled.

'No, sir,' he answered. 'I had to deliver a message for Miss Latimer to one of the stewards — Major Briscoe — a great friend of Lord Latimer's, sir.'

'I hope you took advantage of the opportunity and backed a winner,' said Vicky.

'Yes, thank you, madam,' replied Masters. 'I had a small amount on Summer Lightning — 'Tich' Dukes's mount. He is a very *lucky* jockey, don't you think? One hopes that his luck will not desert him. Good afternoon, madam. Good afternoon, gentlemen.'

He bowed again and walked away. Gordon looked after him, thoughtfully.

'I wonder what exactly he meant by that?' he said, softly. 'You'd almost think he knew something, wouldn't you?'

IV

Mr. Budd, Gordon Cross and Vicky sat drinking coffee in the living-room of Cross's flat. They had persuaded the big superintendent to come in for a rest and a meal before going back to the Yard.

'Well,' said Mr. Budd, leaning back comfortably in his chair, 'it's five hours since the Tipster telephoned the *Clarion*, an' Dukes is still alive.'

'We hope!' remarked Gordon.

Mr. Budd regarded him from under heavy lids.

'If anythin' 'ad gone wrong I'd've 'eard from those two fellers,' he said. ''E's failed this time to carry out his threat.'

'He didn't make any time limit, did he?' said Gordon.

'No, but I don't see 'ow 'e's goin' to get

past my men . . . '

'I hope you're right,' said Gordon, but his tone was not very optimistic.

'Would you like some more coffee, Mr. Budd?' asked Vicky.

'Thank you, Mrs. Cross.' He passed her his empty cup. 'Those two fellers 'ave stuck to Dukes like glue all day an' two others is relievin' 'em an' stoppin' with 'im in his flat all night. 'Ow *can* anythin' 'appen to 'im?'

'I don't know.' Gordon shook his head. 'Perhaps nothing will. I wouldn't be too sure, that's all . . . '

'Gordon thinks the Tipster's omnipotent, Mr. Budd,' said Vicky, as she poured out the coffee.

'If 'e can get at 'Tich' Dukes, I'll agree with 'im,' grunted Mr. Budd.

'I hope you won't have to,' said Gordon. 'You know, Vicky, that idea of yours that something to do with racing is at the bottom of this business looks as if it might be right . . . '

'My ideas are always right, darling,' she said sweetly. She held out the full cup of coffee to Mr. Budd and he took it with a murmured 'thank you.'

'Latimer, Crawford, Dukes — they're all connected with racing,' went on Gordon, thoughtfully.

'If we could find any other connection between 'em, we might be gettin' somewhere,' said Mr. Budd gloomily.

'Yes, that's the snag, isn't it?' agreed Gordon. 'The motive . . . I've racked my brains, but I can't think of anything that's plausible . . . '

'Maybe there isn't one,' said Mr. Budd.

'You mean he's just a homicidal maniac?' said Vicky.

'Well, maybe . . . ' Mr. Budd shrugged his broad shoulders.

'With a hatred for racing?' Gordon made an expressive grimace. 'It doesn't convince *me*. There's something more if we could only find it.'

Mr. Budd sighed, gulped his coffee, and put down the cup and saucer.

'Seems ter me,' he said, 'there's a lot we want ter find — the truth about that 'andkerchief f'instance . . . '

'That's not going to be so easy,' said Gordon. 'Lydia Kenwood admitted that it was hers, but that she'd lost several like it at odd times . . . '

'We've only her word for that, darling,' put in Vicky.

'It'd be a very peculiar coincidence, wouldn't it?' remarked Mr. Budd, 'if one o' those 'andkerchiefs she says she lost should 'ave come into the possession of the Tipster?'

'That depends on *who* the Tipster is, doesn't it?' said Gordon.

'Meanin' that it'ud be queer if 'e should 'appen to be a stranger,' said the big man, 'but not so queer if he was somebody we know?'

'Exactly.'

'Well, that would rule Mr. Kenwood out as a suspect, wouldn't it?' said Vicky. 'He'd hardly use one of his own sister's handkerchiefs . . . '

Gordon shook his head.

'Not necessarily,' he declared. 'He may not have intended to leave it behind. If it had somehow got into his pocket and he was searching for something to wipe that knife with . . . '

'That'd be possible,' said Mr. Budd.

'But careless,' said Vicky. 'Carelessness doesn't appear to be one of the Tipster's failings . . . '

'You think the 'andkerchief was planted?' asked Mr. Budd.

'Yes, I do,' she said. 'Maurice Swayne could have got hold of it easily enough. He knows the Kenwoods . . . '

'So could Kenwood — and Masters . . . ' put in Gordon.

'*Masters*?' She sounded incredulous.

'That was a very strange remark he made this afternoon . . . '

'I don't think he meant anything,' said Vicky. 'Dukes has had a lot of wins this season — that's all he was referring to. It just happened to fit, that's all.'

'I expect he knew Dukes 'ad been threatened,' said Mr. Budd. 'That feller was in such a state of funk that I bet 'e told everybody. Masters couldn't have put through that first call to the *Clarion*, any'ow. 'E was in the pictures . . . '

'The girl in the box-office saw him go *in*,' interrupted Gordon, 'but there's nothing to have stopped him leaving again by one of the side exits, putting through that call and, later, calling into the *Compasses* for a drink . . . '

'There's something in *that*,' said Mr. Budd, nodding. 'I'll 'ave ter . . . '

The clock on the mantelpiece chimed the quarter-past seven and he broke off with an exclamation.

'I must be goin',' he said, getting heavily to his feet. 'I've still got some work to do at the Yard before I can go 'ome . . . '

He said 'good night' and Gordon escorted him to the door. When he came back Vicky was collecting the dirty coffee cups.

'Vicky,' he said, lighting a cigarette, 'how would you like a night out?'

She looked up from the tray in surprise.

'What sort of a night out?' she demanded, suspiciously.

'Oh, drinks and dancing — supper — the usual thing,' he said.

'I'd love it.'

'Well, get your things on then,' he said.

' 'Where are we going?' she asked.

'To the Odds On — old Jacob

Bellamy's place,' he answered. 'Remember him? He used to be a bookie before he retired and opened his club . . . '

'I remember him.' She nodded. 'Why are we going, darling? It's no good telling me it's just for pleasure, because I wouldn't believe it . . . '

'Well, as a matter of fact it isn't . . . '

'I thought not,' she answered.

'Jacob Bellamy has been in the racing game all his life,' explained Gordon. 'There's very little about it he doesn't know. I've an idea he might be able to supply us with the link we lack.'

'I don't like the alliteration, darling,' she said. 'You mean what connection there is, if any, between Lord Latimer, James Crawford, and Dukes?'

'The *hidden* connection, Vicky,' he said seriously. 'The motive that brought the Tipster into being.'

5

I

Everybody knows the 'Odds On' that occupies the corner of a narrow street off the upper end of Piccadilly. The majority know it better as 'Bellamy's Place,' and any taxi-driver, given that direction, will drive you unerringly to the not very imposing entrance.

Looked at from this vantage point the Odds On club is not impressive, but once you have passed through its narrow doors you enter a world of soft lights and thick carpets and every luxury that you could desire. The dance floor is larger than most of its kind; the food is well-cooked and served with a deferential deftness that leaves no ground for complaint; the band is one of the best to be found, and the wines are unquestionably of a fine vintage. Of course the Odds On is expensive. You cannot have all these amenities without paying heavily for the privilege, but at least you know, when you go to Bellamy's Place, that you are getting good value for your money.

Francaire, the head waiter, greeted Vicky and Gordon Cross with a welcoming smile that showed all his very white and very even teeth.

'Eet is a very long time since you come 'ere, Mr. Cross,' he said.

'Quite a while, isn't it, Francaire,' said Gordon. His eyes roved over the crowded floor. 'You're pretty full to-night . . . '

'We are always full,' replied Francaire. 'Business is ver' good. But I will find you a table . . . Mrs. Cross — you are looking sharming . . . sharming . . . '

'Thank you . . . That's very nice of you, Francaire,' said Vicky.

The head waiter spread his hands.

'Eet is not always that one can pay the compliment and speak the truth at the same time,' he said. 'Please come this way.' They followed him through the tables at the side of the dance floor. At one of these he stopped, whisked an engaged ticket from it, and pulled out a chair.

'‛Ere you are,' he said. 'Not too near zee band . . . You would like something to drink?'

'I'd like a gin and orange — with a little soda and some ice,' said Vicky. 'Gordon's gin, please . . . '

'Double-Scotch and a dry-ginger for me,' said Gordon.

'I will instruct zee waiter,' said Francaire.

'Is Mr. Bellamy here yet?' asked Gordon.

'He is in 'is office, Mr. Cross. You would like to see 'im? I will tell 'im you are 'ere.'

He bowed and hurried away.

Vicky let her cloak slip off her shoulders and looked round.

'Uhuh,' she sighed happily. 'It's nice to be here, darling . . . '

'I believe you'll purr in a minute, Vicky,' he said.

'Is that a polite way of saying that I'm a cat?' she demanded.

He laughed.

'No — just that you look sort of well-fed, contented, and sleek,' he said.

'You're not as good as Francaire at compliments,' she said.

'I might be, if my job depended on it,' he retorted.

'Do you know,' she said, 'this is the first time you've taken me out for over a month?'

'Is it?' said Gordon. 'We must make up for it when this business is over . . . '

'I've heard *that* one before, darling,' she said.

'Gin and orange, madam? Whisky and ginger-ale, sir?' The waiter took the glasses from his tray and set them down on the table. 'Anything else, sir?'

'No, thank you,' said Gordon. He picked up his glass. 'Down the hatch, Vicky . . . '

'Cheerio,' she said.

The band began a new number and he looked at her inquiringly.

'Like to dance?'

She nodded.

'Enjoying yourself?' he asked as they mingled with the throng on the dance floor.

'Yes.' She smiled up at him. 'You're

quite a good dancer, you know, darling.'

'Considering I don't get much practice, I don't think I'm so bad, myself,' he replied modestly.

'Well!' She made a grimace. 'Nobody could say you suffered from an inferiority complex, Gordon Cross.'

As they came round near the entrance a girl came in and Vicky gave a little surprised exclamation.

'Gordon,' she whispered. 'Look . . . do you see who's just come in?'

He followed the direction of her eyes and his face changed. 'Iris Latimer,' he murmured.

'Queer she should come to a place like this — so soon after her father . . . '

'Alone, too,' he interrupted.

'She's not alone,' said Vicky quickly. 'Look, she's joined that elderly man — at the table in the corner . . . '

'Strange-looking bloke,' said Gordon. 'Not the type you'd expect Iris Latimer to be friendly with . . . Let's go back and sit down, Vicky . . . '

He led the way back to their table.

'Well,' remarked his wife, as they sat

down, 'that was short, if it wasn't very sweet.'

'I don't want Iris Latimer to see us if it can be helped,' he said. 'I'd like . . . Here comes Jacob . . . '

The huge figure of old Jacob Bellamy loomed up through the crowd of dancers.

' 'Ullo, cock — 'ullo, m'dear,' he greeted, in his rough, husky voice, his wooden face beaming with pleasure at the sight of them. 'Well, well, ain't seen yer for a month o' Sundays.'

'You're looking well, Jacob,' said Gordon, as the ex-bookmaker pulled out a chair and sat down.

'Mustn't grumble,' said Jacob Bellamy. 'Wotcher doin', you two? 'Avin' a night out?'

'Well, not exactly, Jacob,' said Gordon. 'I suppose you've heard of — the Tipster?'

'Cor blimey!' Bellamy looked quickly from one to the other. ' 'Ave you got yerself mixed up with *that*, cock?'

'I'm going to find out what's behind it,' said Gordon. 'That's why we're here. I believe you can help . . . '

'*Me?*' Jacob Bellamy looked surprised.

'There's not much that goes on you don't know about, you old scoundrel,' said Gordon, 'particularly in the racing world. What I'm trying to find is the motive at the back of these murders. It's something to do with racing and it's something that involves Latimer, Crawford and Dukes . . . '

'Dukes?' broke in the old man. 'D'yer mean 'Tich' Dukes — the jockey?'

'Yes, he's the third person the Tipster's after. He hasn't got him yet . . . '

' 'Tich' Dukes, eh?' Bellamy's big face darkened. 'Well, I for one wouldn't be sorry ter see the little rat bumped off . . . '

'Why?' asked Vicky.

' 'E's the crookedest rider that ever cocked a leg over a saddle — that's why,' declared Jacob Bellamy. 'Blimey — I ain't bin no saint in my time — never pretended ter be, but I allus tried ter keep racin' clean. Dukes 'ud sell 'is own mother if 'e was paid enough.'

'That's interesting,' said Gordon. 'Crawford's reputation wasn't too good either, was it?'

'Good?' echoed old Jacob scornfully. ' 'E was another perisher what ought ter

112

'ave been 'warned off' years ago . . . '

'What about Latimer?' asked Gordon.

'Ah, now 'e was a gen'l'man,' said the ex-book-maker. 'A real sportsman. There's plenty like 'im in racin', cock. It's the rabble like Crawford an' 'Tich' Dukes what spoils it an' gets it a bad name. This Tipster chap 'ud be doin' a bit o' good if 'e wiped all them kind out . . . '

He made an expressive gesture with a huge hand that was nearly as big as a leg of mutton.

'It would be a rather drastic way of cleaning up the sport, Jacob,' said Gordon. 'After all, murder is murder . . . '

'I s'pose yer right, boy,' agreed the old man, 'but these twisters allus make me see red. Are you working fer the *Clarion*?'

'Not yet,' said Gordon, 'but I hope to be if I get the inside story of this business.'

'Ah, I see, cock,' said Bellamy shrewdly. 'Well, I'll do all I can to 'elp yer . . . '

'Thank you, Jacob.'

' . . . Though I can't see 'ow I can do much. This feller ain't got Dukes yet, yer say?'

Gordon shook his head.

'There's s'posed ter be two more arter 'im, ain't there?' asked Bellamy thoughtfully.

'Yes. Five people, Jacob,' said Gordon. 'Three definitely connected with the turf and the other two most probably. Five people that the Tipster wants to kill for some reason — and two of whom he has *already* killed . . . What did they do to *him*, Jacob?'

'Blimey!' said Bellamy. 'Now yer askin', boy, ain't yer? You think this feller's gettin' back on 'em for somethin' they done to 'im?'

'It sounds logical, doesn't it, Mr. Bellamy?' said Vicky.

'I don't know much about logic, m'dear,' answered the old man, 'but if that's yer idea why not 'ave a dekko inter their pasts? . . . yer might find somethin' that applies ter *all* of 'em . . . '

'That's what I thought *you* might do, Jacob,' said Gordon. 'You've been in the racing game all your life. You know everybody. Think back over the history of these three people and try and remember some point — some *big* point — where their lives all touch . . . '

'Yer know, cock, yer gettin' me interested,' said Bellamy.

Gordon winked at Vicky.

'That,' he said, 'is what I wanted to do . . . '

'Well, I'll do me best, cock, but don't you go thinkin' that it's a cert. I may not be able ter turn up anythin'.'

'I'm sure if anybody can, you can, Mr. Bellamy,' said Vicky, sweetly.

'Bin kissin' the blarney stone, ain't yer, Vick?' growled the old man, but his eyes twinkled. 'You needn't pull that stuff on me, gal. I tell yer what though,' he added, seriously, 'if I 'elp yer, yer've got ter let me in on any excitement that's goin'?'

'I'll promise you that, Jacob,' said Gordon.

'Blimey! I could do with a bit o' excitement, cock,' said the old man. 'Gettin' stale, I am, watchin' people eatin' an' drinkin' and dancin' night after night an' listenin' ter this ruddy stuff they calls music. The money rolls in but I wouldn't 'alf like a good old scrap with the 'boys'

115

— like the old days . . . '

His huge hands clenched and his eyes sparkled at the memories he had conjured up.

'You're a bloodthirsty old ruffian,' chuckled Gordon.

'Iris Latimer and that man are going,' said Vicky suddenly.

'Iris Latimer?' Bellamy swung round quickly. 'Is she 'ere?'

'Yes . . . Who's the man with her?'

'I don't know, m'dear. I've never set eyes on 'im before,' said Bellamy. 'Queer lookin' bloke, ain't 'e?' His voice changed suddenly. 'That feller what's just come in's a slimy rat. I've told 'im before I don't want 'im 'ere . . . 'Scuse me.' He got hastily to his feet and began to make his way quickly through the tables. Gordon looked round to see what had upset the old man and saw that Maurice Swayne had come in.

'H'm,' he remarked, 'Mr. Maurice Swayne doesn't appear to be very welcome, Vicky.'

'I'm not surprised,' she said. 'Why the Kenwoods put up with him, I can't imagine.'

'Perhaps they can't help themselves,' he answered, a little absently. 'Vicky, I'm sure I've seen that man with Iris Latimer somewhere before . . . '

'Where?'

He shook his head.

'I don't know . . . I'm trying to remember . . . '

'Mr. Bellamy is having a terrific argument with Swayne,' she said. 'You can't see from where you're sitting . . . '

'That's it,' he exclaimed suddenly. 'That day in the police court when Swayne was brought up for blackmail . . . The case before his was one of assault. A man was charged with half killing another man in Soho . . . '

'Gordon . . . You mean . . . ?'

'Yes . . . that man, who's just left with Iris Latimer, was the man in the dock.'

II

Gordon Cross brought the car skilfully into the kerb and stopped.

'You go on up, Vicky,' he said. 'I'll take

this bus back to the garage. I shan't be long . . . '

She gathered up her skirts and got out.

'All right,' she said, yawning. 'Oh, I'm so tired, darling . . . '

'Get straight into bed,' he said. 'I'll make some tea and bring it in to you . . . '

'I don't think I can keep awake long enough to drink it,' she answered. 'Don't be long, darling . . . '

She crossed the strip of pavement as he drove away and entered the dark vestibule of the flats. There was no night porter. The block was an old-fashioned one with a stone staircase that led from the main entrance to the front doors of the various flats. The luxury of a light was something that the builders had not considered necessary.

Vicky mounted the dark stairs slowly, humming one of the dance tunes that the band had played at the Odds On. She was so tired that she could scarcely find her key and had to fumble in her bag for a long time before she finally located it. Pushing it into the lock she turned it and opened the front door. Her hand was on the switch just inside the hall when a voice spoke out of the darkness — a queer nasal voice that was somehow — horrible . . .

'Don't put on the light, Mrs. Cross . . . '

She gave a startled cry and fell back against the door frame.

'Who's there,' she gasped. 'Who is it?'

'The Tipster,' was the reply.

She felt as if all the muscles in her throat had contracted as a hand gripped her wrist and pulled her fully inside.

'The Tipster?' she faltered and her voice was dry and rasping and scarcely audible.

'I am varying my usual routine, Mrs. Cross,' the hateful, nasal voice went on out of the darkness. 'Instead of ringing up the *Clarion*, I've decided to give *you* the name of my next — er — 'certainty' for the murder stakes . . . '

'I . . . I thought . . . ' she stammered, almost incoherent with fear, and he interrupted her.

'You are thinking of 'Tich' Dukes?' he said. 'He has already been dealt with . . . '

'You mean . . . he's dead?' she breathed.

'Do you think I should fail?' he

chuckled softly. 'Yes, he's dead.'

'But . . . how?'

'That is of no consequence,' he said, impatiently. 'You have heard of Lewis Tidmann, Mrs. Cross?'

'No . . . '

'Your husband, I am sure, will be better informed,' he said. 'Lewis Tidmann is to be the next. Will you pass my 'information' on, Mrs. Cross? And tell your husband not to be too inquisitive — it might be dangerous.'

Suddenly he was past her and out of the front door. It slammed shut behind him and she heard his footsteps hurrying down the stairs. For a moment she leaned back against the wall, shaking from the shock, and then she wrenched open the door and ran out on to the landing, calling hysterically.

'Gordon . . . Gordon!'

There was no reply and she leaned over the rail, staring down into the well of the staircase. And then she heard footsteps . . .

'Gordon . . . is that you?' she called.

His voice came up to her, faintly but reassuring:

'What is it, darling . . . what's the matter?'

'Gordon . . . he's been here,' she said. 'He was here when I got here . . . '

He came running up the remaining stairs two at a time.

'He?' he demanded. 'Who?'

'The Tipster?' she answered unsteadily.

'*What!*' There was alarm and consternation in his voice.

'He was waiting . . . inside the door . . . in the dark,' quavered Vicky, trembling in his arms. 'He's got a horrible, beastly voice . . . , beastly . . . '

'What did he come for?' asked Gordon.

'He said . . . he said . . . ' She was shaking so violently that she could scarcely speak.

'Steady, Vicky,' he said. 'What you want is a drink . . . Come along into the sitting-room and I'll get you one . . . '

With his arm round her, he led her into the flat. Opening the sitting-room door, he pressed down the light switch.

'Go and sit down, darling,' he said, 'and I'll . . . '

Her scream broke in on the rest of the sentence.

'Gordon . . . look . . . oh, look . . . there on the settee . . . '

He swung round towards the settee drawn up by the empty fireplace. Something was lying there . . . crumpled and unnatural.

'My God!' he whispered. 'It's 'Tich' Dukes!'

6

I

Mr. Budd sat heavy-eyed and weary in the sitting-room of Gordon Cross's flat, gloomily sipping coffee. It was nearly five o'clock and another lovely summer morning, but the stout superintendent was not interested in its beauties. He had been wakened in the middle of the night by a telephone call from Gordon Cross to his small house at Streatham, and when he had heard what the reporter had to tell him, had dressed hurriedly and come post-haste to the Bloomsbury flat. And from then until now he had been a very busy and worried man.

'That's all we can do for the moment,' he remarked, wearily. 'I'll 'ave another cup o' coffee if yer don't mind . . . '

'There isn't any more milk,' said Gordon.

'I'd rather 'ave it black.' Mr. Budd set

down his empty cup and sighed. 'I'm going ter get properly 'carpeted' fer this little packet, Mr. Cross,' he said, shaking his head. 'The A.C. was a bit sticky over Crawford. What 'e's goin' ter say when 'e 'ears about this . . . ' He pursed his thick lips and whistled expressively.

'You did all you could,' said Gordon, pouring out the coffee.

'That won't cut a lot o' ice with the A.C.,' remarked Mr. Budd. 'Results is all that counts with 'im . . . Maybe they'll put somebody else on the case . . . '

'Nonsense,' said Gordon. 'They must realize that the Tipster isn't an ordinary crook — he's unique . . . '

'At rock bottom 'e's the same as any other murderer,' grunted Mr. Budd. 'All the rest is just trimmin's.'

'I suppose you're right,' agreed Gordon, after a moment. 'He's a pretty cool customer, all the same. It took nerve to do what he did to-night.'

'I should 'ave 'ad a man in Dukes's bedroom,' said Mr. Budd, shaking his head. 'But I thought with a feller in the sitting-room an' another outside 'e'd be

124

safe as 'ouses. I never thought the Tipster 'ud take the risk of slippin' up the fire-escape an' gettin' in the winder o' the bedroom . . . '

'I suppose he strangled that poor little devil before he had a chance to wake up and give the alarm?'

Mr. Budd nodded.

'Must've done,' he said. 'Neither o' my men saw or 'eard a thing — not a sound.'

'He must have got into this flat the same way,' remarked Gordon. 'The fire-escape runs up by the kitchen window and we found the window open . . . '

'These fire-escapes!' growled Mr. Budd disgustedly. 'We call 'em 'the burglar's joy.'' He pulled irritably at his nose. 'Wonder why 'e went to the trouble o' gettin' Dukes's body out of 'is own flat an' bringin' it 'ere?'

'Vanity,' said Gordon, 'sheer colossal vanity. It's behind everything he does. All criminals are vain . . . '

'They ain't got it as badly as 'e 'as,' said the big man.

'If I'd only come back a few seconds

sooner from putting that car away, I'd have met him on the stairs.'

'You can thank yer lucky stars yer didn't,' said Mr. Budd grimly. 'You wouldn't be alive now, if you 'ad. Well, I've got to 'and it to 'im, 'e don't make mistakes . . . not a print, not a footmark . . . Not a blessed thing to suggest 'is identity.'

'Except,' said Gordon, slowly, 'Clair de Lune . . . '

'Clair de . . . oh, yer mean that tune?'

'My wife says he was whistling it as he ran down the staircase.'

Mr. Budd was not very impressed.

'That's a lot o' good to us,' he said. 'I know *you* think it's important . . . '

'I do,' declared Gordon. 'I think it's very important.'

'I'd prefer something practical,' said Mr. Budd.

'Well, you've got it,' said Gordon, unexpectedly. 'We know *one* thing about him that we didn't know before . . . '

'What?' The big man opened his eyes very wide.

'He owns a car,' said Gordon. 'He

126

couldn't have brought the body of Dukes here any other way . . . '

Mr. Budd looked disappointed.

'I'm already on to that,' he said. 'I've 'ad a district call sent out asking fer information about any car seen near Dukes's flat an' this one at the time it 'appened.'

'Good. Now what have you done about this man Lewis Tidmann?'

'I've got a detective-inspector an' two men with 'im,' said Mr. Budd. 'I stationed them there meself soon as I got your telephone message . . . An' they won't let 'im out o' their sight. I *daren't* let anythin' 'appen ter Tidmann after *this*. The A.C. 'ud 'ave me coat off me back . . . '

'When are you going to see Tidmann?' asked Gordon.

'Soon as I leave 'ere . . . '

'I'll come with you,' said Gordon.

'What about Mrs. Cross?' asked Mr. Budd. ' 'Ow is she?'

'I gave her a sleeping tablet and made her go to bed. She was fast asleep when I last looked in.'

'Best thin' for 'er,' said the big man,

yawning. 'I'll leave Bailey in the kitchen — just in case . . . '

'You don't think Vicky's in any danger, do you?' said Gordon, anxiously.

'When yer dealin' with a feller like this there's no tellin',' said Mr. Budd. ' 'E knows you're in this, Mr. Cross, an' if 'e thinks you're goin' ter be a nuisance . . . Well, there's no knowing what 'e might do.'

II

'Have a drink, Superintendent?' said Mr. Lewis Tidmann, pouring out a generous helping of John Haig and gulping it down. He was a stout man with an unhealthy flabby face and small eyes that looked out over heavy pouches.

'No, thank yer, sir,' said Mr. Budd.

'What about you, Mr. Cross?' asked Tidmann.

Gordon shook his head and Mr. Tidmann replenished his own glass, and chuckled throatily.

'A man who gets pulled out of his bed

in the middle of the night an' told he's going to be murdered needs something, eh?' he said. 'This man — the Tipster . . . He's mad, of course?'

'It's by no means certain,' said Gordon.

'Of course he is — he must be,' said Mr. Tidmann. 'No sane man 'ud go about killin' people for nothing.' He drank some more whisky and pulled his dressing-gown closer round him. 'But that don't make him any less dangerous. I'm relyin' on the police for protection, Superintendent . . . '

'You're gettin' it, sir,' said Mr. Budd, curtly. He did not like Mr. Lewis Tidmann.

'Well, it had better be more effective than the protection you gave the others,' grunted Mr. Tidmann. 'That wasn't much use, was it?'

'Every precaution will be taken, sir.'

'I don't think I'm more cowardly than the next man,' continued Mr. Tidmann, smoothing his nearly bald head, 'but a feller can't 'ear that he's likely to be bumped off at any minute without getting a bit of a shock, eh?'

'No, sir, naturally,' agreed Mr. Budd. 'Do you know of any reason why this feller should want ter kill you? Can you suggest any motive?'

Mr. Tidmann swallowed some more whisky. His voice, when he answered, was a little slurred.

'Motive? For his wanting to kill *me?* Good Lord, no! There isn't one. He's just plain crazy . . . '

'That's very likely,' agreed Mr. Budd. 'But you realize that we've got to exhaust all other possibilities until we can be sure o' that. If there should be any logical reason for these murders, it 'ud 'elp us greatly ter get a line on the killer.'

''Fraid I can't help you there,' said Tidmann, shaking his head. 'There's no reason why anyone should want ter kill me . . . '

Gordon thought there might be many reasons but he only said: 'You're managing director of Laybets, the turf accountants, aren't you, Mr. Tidmann?'

'That's right,' said Mr. Tidmann.

'You must have a number of clients who lose heavily . . . '

'Dozens of 'em, Mr. Cross,' said Tidmann with a chuckle. '*That* line won't get you anywhere, and what about Latimer, Crawford and Dukes? You can't find a motive that'll fit all of 'em, can you?'

'That's what we are trying to do,' said Cross. 'Lord Latimer was Senior Steward of the Jockey Club, Crawford was a trainer, Dukes was a jockey — you, Mr. Tidmann, are a bookmaker . . . All in the same business — racing. Does that suggest anything to you?'

'You mean something happened to this feller — something for which Latimer, Crawford, Dukes and me are responsible?' grunted Mr. Tidmann.

'And *one* other person,' said Cross. 'The Tipster said there would be *five*.'

'It's fantastic!' Tidmann poured out another Haig. 'If there was anything like that I'd know about it, wouldn't I?'

'Well, that's what we're asking you,' said Cross. 'Can't you think of *anything* in which you could *all* have been involved, that may have seriously harmed — somebody?'

'No — because there isn't anything of the sort,' said Tidmann, impatiently. 'You're trying to find a difficult explanation when a simple one's staring you in the face. This Tipster chap's a loony . . . Don't you agree, Superintendent?'

'Well, o' course, sir, as I've already said, it's possible,' said Mr. Budd cautiously.

'Not committing yourself beyond that, eh?' Tidmann took a drink. His capacity for whisky seemed unlimited. 'Well, loony or no loony, the question is — what steps are you taking to look after *me?* That's the important thing.'

'That's in the 'ands of Detective-sergeant Porter, sir,' said Mr. Budd. ' 'E'll see that you don't go anywhere durin' the day unguarded, an' at night a detective'll keep watch in yer bedroom . . . '

'Bit awkward if I was a married man, eh?' remarked the bookmaker with a chuckle. 'Sure you two won't have a snifter?' His hand went out to the bottle of Haig.

They both declined.

'Haven't you got any clue to the identity of this feller?' Tidmann went on.

'It seems incredible to me that he could have committed — how many murders? — three, without leaving some trace behind.'

'Well, nuthin' that you could really call a clue,' began Mr. Budd.

'Only a tune, Mr. Tidmann,' put in Gordon Cross. 'Just after Lord Latimer was killed somebody was heard whistling 'Clair de Lune' . . . '

'Well, that's not much to go on,' began Tidmann, and then his voice broke and he added quickly: '*What* did you say it was called?'

'Clair de Lune,' repeated Gordon.

'Clair de Lune,' breathed Tidmann. The colour left his face and he gulped the remainder of his whisky quickly.

'Does it convey anything to you?' asked Cross.

'No . . . ' Tidmann recovered himself by an effort, but the hand that held the empty glass was shaking. 'No . . . nothing . . . '

'My wife heard the man who called himself the Tipster whistling the same tune as he ran away down the stairs . . . '

The glass fell from Mr. Tidmann's hand and rolled on the carpet . . . 'Is anything the matter?'

'No . . . no . . . ' muttered the bookmaker huskily. 'Just — just a twinge of rheumatism, Mr. Cross, that's all.'

III

'That excuse about rheumatism was all my eye and Betty Martin,' said Gordon, when they left Mr. Tidmann's flat. 'It was the mention of 'Clair de Lune' that upset him.'

'Maybe you're right,' grunted Mr. Budd.

'I'm sure of it,' declared Gordon. 'He suddenly remembered something — something that the mention of that tune called up — and it wasn't a very pleasant memory . . . '

'If it was anythin' likely to give us a line on the Tipster why didn't 'e tell us?' demanded Mr. Budd.

Gordon shrugged his shoulders.

'Perhaps it was something he *couldn't*

tell us,' he said significantly. 'Look, there's a restaurant open over there — let's see if they can give us some breakfast. I'm starving . . . '

The restaurant not only could, but did, provide them with an excellent breakfast of kippers, bread and butter, toast and marmalade, and tea. When they had finished and Gordon was smoking a cigarette, Mr. Budd suddenly leaned forward.

'I've been thinkin',' he said. 'Could this tune 'ave somethin' ter do with a woman, Mr. Cross? 'Clair de Lune' — Claire's a woman's name, ain't it?'

'*That* hadn't struck me,' said Gordon, nodding. 'It's certainly an idea . . . '

'There's mostly a woman be'ind anythin' like this, if you dig deep enough,' grunted the big man, pouring himself out another cup of tea.

'*Cherchez la femme*, eh?' Gordon grinned across at him.

'If you'd 'ad my experience you'd realize that it's a pretty sound principle, Mr. Cross . . . '

'A woman *could* be the link between

135

these people,' agreed Gordon thoughtfully.

'An' if she was the wife or the gal friend of this Tipster feller,' augmented Mr. Budd, 'an' somethin' 'ad 'appened to her due to these five people — that'd supply a good motive, wouldn't it?'

'Yes — undoubtedly it would,' said Gordon.

'It's worth workin' on,' said Mr. Budd complacently. He was pleased with his theory.

'It doesn't have to be a wife or girl friend, you know,' said Gordon. 'Any close relation would fit the bill — a sister, for instance.'

Mr. Budd eyed him shrewdly.

'If yer thinkin' of Kenwood, Mr. Cross,' he said slowly, ' 'is sister's name is Lydia.'

'She has another,' replied Gordon. 'The initials on her handbag are L.C.K. I wonder what the C stands for?'

Mr. Budd rose ponderously to his feet.

'I think,' he remarked, 'it might be worth while to find out . . . '

Gordon went back to his flat and as he turned the key in the lock of the front door Vicky's voice called him from the bedroom.

'Is that you, Gordon?'

'Yes, darling.' He shut the door. 'How are you feeling now?'

'Come in here,' she invited, and he went into the bedroom. 'Where have you been?'

'With Budd to see Lewis Tidmann,' he answered. 'We stopped to have breakfast afterwards . . . '

Vicky sat up, pulling the bed-clothes up round her chin.

'There's a man in the kitchen, Gordon . . . ' she began.

'I know,' he interrupted, 'he's a detective. Budd thought it would be safer . . . '

'Oh, I see.' She nodded. 'How is Tidmann?'

'Well, he's still alive,' if that's what you mean,' he answered.

'What did he say — when you told him?' she asked.

'Nothing very much. But I'm sure he knows something, Vicky. When we told him about the Tipster's signature tune, it gave him quite a shock. He pretended it didn't, but I know it did . . . What are you going to do?'

'I'm getting up,' she answered calmly. 'Give me my dressing-gown, please . . . '

'I don't think you ought to . . . ' he began.

'Rubbish!' she retorted. 'There's nothing the matter with me . . . Run the bath, darling, and don't fuss . . . '

'Fuss!' he repeated indignantly. 'Well, I like that! I was only thinking that it would be better if . . . '

'If you could keep me quietly in bed while you go chasing about on your own,' she finished.

'I never thought . . . '

'I'm in this and I'm not going to be left out of any of the excitement, Gordon Cross.'

'Haven't you had enough — after last night?' he demanded.

'No . . . ' She slipped out of bed and put on her dressing-gown. 'Now run the bath, there's a . . . '

The telephone began ringing in the sitting-room and Gordon frowned.

'Who the devil is that?' he muttered.

His wife gave him a dazzling smile.

'It's not a bad idea, darling,' she said sweetly, 'to pick up the receiver and find out.'

He made a rude gesture and hurried into the sitting-room. When he picked up the receiver a man's voice came urgently over the wire.

'Mr. Cross?' it said.

'Yes . . . who is . . . ?'

'This is Masters, sir,' the voice went on quickly. 'Would it be possible to see you, sir? This morning . . . about eleven?'

'What is it, Masters?'

'I can't explain over the telephone, sir,' said Masters. 'It's very important. Could you manage to come to Newbury? I could meet you at the *Compasses*, sir . . . '

'Why the *Compasses*?' asked Gordon.

'I'll explain when I see you, sir,' said Masters. 'It . . . it's *very* urgent, sir . . . '

'All right — I'll come,' said Gordon.

'Thank you, sir.' There was a click as Masters hung up the telephone, and Gordon replaced the receiver thoughtfully. What did Masters want with him so urgently? And why couldn't he have made the appointment at the house?

He went back to the bedroom but Vicky was no longer there. He called her and a muffled voice answered him from behind the closed door of the bathroom.

'I'm in here . . . Who was it?'

'Masters,' he replied. 'He wants to see me urgently. I'm going to Newbury . . . '

'I won't be long . . . '

'I said I'd go at once . . . '

'You dare to go without me, Gordon Cross,' she called indignantly.

'But I can't wait,' he protested.

'If you don't,' declared Vicky, 'I'll . . . I'll divorce you . . . '

'Be quiet,' he said, suddenly remembering the man in the kitchen. 'The detective will hear you . . . '

'Good,' she retorted, 'I'll scream for help and tell him you're ill-treating me . . . He can be a witness . . . '

'Oh, all right,' he said resignedly. 'How long are you going to be?'

'I'll be ready, darling,' she said sweetly, 'by the time you've brought the car round'

IV

The morning was lovely. The car which Gordon Cross had borrowed from the garage was an ancient model, but it went, if the going was not particularly fast and furious.

'We branch off somewhere here for the *Compasses*, don't we?' asked Gordon, as they came to the outskirts of Newbury.

Vicky nodded.

'It's that road that dips steeply, I think,' she said. 'Don't you remember, darling? Just before you turn off for Latimer's place. I wonder why Masters is so anxious to see you?'

'You've already said that *five* times, Vicky,' he remarked. 'How should I know?'

'Well, I'm curious,' she said. 'Why should he suggest meeting you at the *Compasses* — why couldn't we go to the house?'

'Your guess is as good as mine,' he answered. 'Here we are. This is where we turn off, isn't it?'

'I think so,' she said. 'Yes that's right.'

The car turned into a narrow lane that dipped steeply between thick woodland that grew on either side. The branches of the huge trees met and interlaced overhead so that only patches of sunlight filtered through. It was very pretty and the shade was a relief from the blazing sun which had beaten down pitilessly on the roof of the car and made the interior unpleasantly hot in spite of the open windows.

'Gordon,' said Vicky, suddenly, 'supposing *Masters* is the Tipster?'

'How did you come by that bright idea?' said Gordon.

'It would account for the handkerchief, wouldn't it?' she said. 'Masters could easily have got hold of one of Lydia Kenwood's handkerchiefs . . . '

'The same reasoning applies to Kenwood,' he answered.

'Yes, but,' she began, and then: 'Oh, look, Gordon . . . There's somebody in the wood . . . '

'Where? I can't see . . . '

'You're looking to the wrong side,' she said. 'There, do you . . . '

There came a sharp, whip-like report and the back window of the car splintered.

'Gordon!' cried the startled Vicky.

'Are you hurt?' he asked.

Another shot rang out, followed by another and another. A small hole suddenly appeared in the roof.

'Get down, Vicky,' snapped Gordon, urgently. 'Get down . . . He's behind that tree . . . '

Two more shots came in quick succession and the windscreen shattered.

'The swine!' grated Gordon between his teeth. 'Keep down, darling. I'm going to rush it . . . '

He put his foot down hard on the accelerator and the ancient car responded valiantly. Rattling and bumping it sped down the lane at nearly sixty miles an hour, and presently Gordon pulled it up with a screaming protest from the brake drums.

'I think we're out of range now,' he said. 'Phew! . . . That was hot while it lasted . . . Cigarette?'

'Please,' said Vicky shakily. 'What happened?'

'That fellow shot at us from the wood.' Gordon gave her a cigarette, took one

143

himself and lighted both. He twisted round in his seat and examined the damage.

'One bullet through the windscreen and another through the side window,' he said. 'H'm . . . pretty sound shooting at a moving target . . . '

'You mean . . . somebody tried to . . . ?'

'Of course. Neat little ambush, wasn't it? Well, there's the answer to your question, Vicky. We know, now, why Masters was so anxious for us to come to Newbury.'

V

There was nobody in the long bar at the *Compasses* when they arrived. The blonde barmaid was making her face up in a lazy, half-hearted manner, as though even this was a bore.

Gordon ordered a gin and orange for Vicky and a John Haig for himself, and carried the drinks over to a table in the corner.

'Do you think he'll come?' said Vicky.

'Why shouldn't he?' asked Gordon. 'There's nothing to connect him with the shooting. If he *didn't* turn up it would look suspicious.'

'It might *not* have been Masters after all, you know,' said Vicky, frowning. 'Supposing it was somebody who knew Masters had made this appointment — that he was going to tell us something important — and wanted to stop us seeing him?'

'I thought you'd made up your mind that Masters is the Tipster?' he remarked grinning at her.

'I never said he is,' she protested. 'I only said supposing?'

'You'd make a good weathercock, darling,' he said.

She opened her mouth to make a suitable retort to this but the opening of the bar door and the arrival of a customer stopped her.

It was David Kenwood.

'Good morning, Alice,' he said to the blonde barmaid, who gave him a sickly smile.

'Good morning, Mr. Kenwood,' she said in an affected drawl. 'Isn't it hot?'

'Bit too hot for me,' he answered. 'Got any bitter?'

'Only mild and bitter — sorry,' she answered.

'All right, give me a pint of that,' he said.

'Gordon,' whispered Vicky. 'Do you see what he's carrying under his arm?'

He nodded. He had already seen the small, repeating rifle that Kenwood carried.

'Good morning, Mr. Kenwood,' he called across the bar, and Kenwood turned with a start.

'Oh . . . hello, Cross,' he said in apparent surprise. 'Didn't see you in that corner. Good morning, Mrs. Cross.'

'Been — shooting, Mr. Kenwood?' asked Gordon.

'Just a pot shot here and there,' replied Kenwood. 'Swarms of rabbits about this district . . . '

'I shouldn't have thought a rifle was the best gun to use,' said Gordon.

Kenwood laughed.

'It's more sporting. Makes the little beggars more difficult to hit,' he said.

146

'Would you say that either Vicky or me bore the slightest resemblance to rabbits?' asked Gordon, and Kenwood stared.

'What do you mean?' he asked.

'Somebody took a few pot shots at us a little while ago from the wood at the side of the road,' explained Gordon.

'Good heavens,' ejaculated Kenwood. 'The careless fool . . . '

'There was nothing careless about it, Mr. Kenwood,' said Vicky. 'It was far too accurate to be pleasant.'

'You . . . you don't mean that — that it was *intentional*?' demanded Kenwood aghast.

'I most certainly do,' declared Gordon.

'But . . . who?'

'We didn't actually see who it was, but I've a pretty good idea.'

'Who?' asked Kenwood quickly.

'The Tipster,' said Gordon. 'He objects to inquisitive people, Mr. Kenwood. Have another drink?'

'You have one with me,' said Kenwood. He ordered a Gordon's gin and orange for Vicky and a Haig for Gordon. 'Have you told the police about this, Cross?' he asked, as he brought over the drinks.

Gordon shook his head.

'No, not yet,' he answered.

A man came quickly into the bar.

'Double whisky, please miss,' he ordered, and Vicky looked significantly at her husband. The newcomer was the man whom Iris Latimer had come to meet at the Odds On club.

He swallowed his whisky at a gulp, gave a quick glance round, and went out. Kenwood finished his drink, refused another, and pleading that he had to get back, left too.

Vicky and Gordon sat on, but there was no sign of Masters.

'If I drink another gin and orange I shall be tight,' she said at last. 'What are we going to do?'

'Well, it doesn't look as if Masters were coming, does it?' he said.

She shook her head.

'I told you he wouldn't,' she said.

He frowned.

'I don't understand it,' he muttered.

'Perhaps he couldn't get away,' she suggested.

'More likely it was just a ruse to get us into that ambush,' he said. 'But even then I should have thought he would have put in an appearance. It's particularly admitting that he . . . ' He got up quickly. 'I'm going to ring up and see if he's at the house,' he said. He went over to the bar. 'Is there a telephone here?'

The blonde barmaid, who was languidly painting her finger-nails, looked up heavily.

'Through that door — just along the passage,' she said.

'Thank you,' said Gordon. 'I won't be a minute, Vicky.'

When he had gone, Vicky strolled over to the bar.

'You're not very busy, are you?' she said.

'No,' replied the blonde barmaid, waggling her fingers about in the air to dry the scarlet lacquer. ' 'Cept week-ends. We're always full up then.'

'Have you still got Mr. Swayne staying with you?'

'Mr. Swayne? No, he left this morning — soon after breakfast. Is he a friend of yours?'

'No,' said Vicky, 'I wouldn't exactly call him a friend . . . '

'Nasty, smarmy sort o' feller *I* think,' declared the blonde barmaid. 'I'm glad he's gone. Creeping in an' out half the night . . . '

'Did he do that?' asked Vicky. 'You don't know what time he came in *last* night I suppose?'

The barmaid patted her blonde hair, glancing sideways at herself in the mirror at the back of the bar.

'Well, as it happens I do,' she said, 'because the noise of the car woke me up and I looked out of the window to see what it was. My room faces the front, you see . . . '

'Was it very late?'

'No, it was very early,' said the blonde barmaid. 'About five minutes past four this morning . . . '

Gordon came back hurriedly and he looked worried.

'Masters isn't at the house,' he said. 'He went out immediately after breakfast and hasn't been back since.'

'Swayne left this morning too — about

the same time . . . '

'Swayne? Do you mean for good?'

'Yes — and this girl says he didn't come back here until after four this morning . . . '

'At midnight he was at the Odds On . . . '

Vicky nodded.

'I was wondering,' she said meaningly, 'where he was after that . . . '

'You think it might have been — at our flat?'

'Yes . . . '

There was a sudden interruption. The door of the bar was flung violently open and a man came in. He was breathing heavily and looked as though he had been running.

'Alice,' he cried, jerkily. 'Can . . . I use yer phone . . . I want ter get the p'lice . . . '

'The police,' exclaimed the blonde barmaid. 'Whatever is the matter, Mr. Jenkins?'

Mr. Jenkins — he looked like a labourer of some sort — wiped his mouth with the back of his hand.

'There's a dead man . . . at the bottom of the old quarry . . . '

'A dead man,' exclaimed the barmaid, in horrified relish. 'You mean an accident . . . '

'It don't look like no accident to me,' said Jenkins. 'This chap 'ad 'ad his 'ead bashed in with a stone . . . I wouldn't swear to it but I think it was the feller that worked at the Latimers' place — butler, wasn't it?'

'You mean — Mr. Masters . . . ' said the blonde barmaid.

Gordon looked at Vicky.

'So *that*'s why he never kept his appointment,' he whispered.

7

I

They stood on the lip of the old quarry in the hot sunshine, and looked down into its scorching depths. Waves of heat seemed to rise up from the glaring whiteness and engulf them . . .

'Whereabouts is this man, Jenkins?' asked Gordon. 'I can't see any sign . . . '

'Yer can't from 'ere, sir,' said Jenkins. 'It's down by them scrubby bushes.'

'How do we get down?'

'I'll show yer, sir — foller me.'

He began to move gingerly down a steep incline and they followed him with difficulty.

'Mind 'ow you go, sir,' said Jenkins, as Gordon slipped. 'It's easy to twist yer ankle on them loose stones.'

'You're telling me,' said Gordon. 'Surely there's a better way down?'

'There used to be, sir, but part o' the

lip o' the quarry fell in about a year ago an' carried away the path. It's mostly sheer now, 'cept this bit.'

'Give me your hand, Gordon,' called Vicky. 'These high heels are difficult . . . oh . . . '

'Look out,' warned her husband. 'You shouldn't have come. You ought to have stayed at the top . . . '

'You're not leaving me out of it,' said Vicky determinedly.

They slithered and slid for what seemed hours and then Jenkins said:

'Nearly at the bottom now, sir.'

'Thank heaven for that,' gasped Gordon fervently. 'This isn't the ideal weather for this job . . . '

'I'm down,' called Vicky. 'You can jump the rest, Gordon.'

He did, and mopped his face.

'Phew, I'm baking,' he said. 'Now, where did you find this man, Jenkins?'

'T'other side, sir,' said Jenkins. 'Where the quarry rises up almost straight . . . '

'Come on then — let's go . . . '

It was rough going. The bottom of the quarry was uneven and tangled in brambles.

'Gordon,' said Vicky. 'Mr. Budd will never get down here.'

'He'll have to, somehow,' said Gordon. 'Wonder how long it'll take him to get here? He said he'd leave at once, and it's about half an hour since I phoned . . . '

'He can't get here yet, darling,' said Vicky. 'Not unless he comes by plane . . . '

Jenkins, more sure-footed than they, had gone on ahead and now he stopped and turned.

'Here it is, sir,' he called. 'Over here . . . '

He pointed to a clump of bushes. They drew level with him and now they could see . . . The body lay close by the bushes which had screened it from view until they were close to it.

'Them's the clothes that butler chap allus wore, sir,' said Jenkins, 'ain't they?'

Gordon looked down at the thing that lay there. The black coat and striped trousers were definitely Masters's. There was a small, neatly darned tear on the right leg that Gordon remembered . . .

'It's Masters right enough,' said Gordon, huskily. 'Don't look, Vicky . . . It's rather nasty . . . His head's been battered almost to pulp . . . with that big stone, by the look of it . . . '

Vicky turned her head away. She was sorry she had seen anything of that horrible sight. It had made her feel sick . . . the hot sun and the flies . . . Gordon saw the whiteness of her face and gently led her away.

'I told you, you shouldn't have come,' he said. 'We'd better not touch anything until Budd arrives . . . '

'You want me to wait, sir?' said Jenkins, scratching his head.

'I'm afraid you'll have to,' said Gordon. 'I don't think it will be very long before . . . '

'What's that?' broke in Vicky, suddenly.

'What?'

'That . . . glistening in the sun — close by your foot?'

He followed the direction of her pointing finger and saw it — a glistening pin-point in the dust. Stooping, he picked up a tie-pin — a small diamond set in a clenched fist of gold. He stared at it, frowning.

'Now where have I seen *that* before?' he muttered.

Vicky came over and looked at it.

'I can tell you,' she said. 'In Maurice Swayne's tie.'

II

It was cool in the long drawing-room at White Gables — a delicious coolness that was restful to eyes aching from the hot glare and dust of the quarry. Mr. Budd, his big face the colour of a newly-baked brick and glistening with tiny drops of perspiration, sat in an armchair, his heavy eyes half-closed.

He had succeeded, with a great deal of labour and the expenditure of much breath, in descending into the quarry. That had been child's play compared with the difficulty he had had in getting out of it again, and he had reached White Gables in a state of exhaustion.

'There's no doubt about it at all, Miss Latimer,' he remarked, looking sleepily across at Iris. 'Your butler, Masters, was murdered. 'E wasn't only killed, 'e was savagely battered about the face an' 'ead. It's my opinion, an' the opinion of the doctor, that 'e was flung into the quarry an' the murderer then climbed down an' made certain 'e was dead . . . '

'Why?' she asked, in a low voice, 'why should anyone do such a horrible thing?'

'Because Masters knew somethin', miss,' grunted Mr. Budd, 'an' the murderer wanted to stop 'im *tellin'* what 'e knew . . . '

'You think the murderer was this man — the Tipster?' asked David Kenwood. He and his sister had been with Iris Latimer when they had arrived with the news.

'Yes, Mr. Kenwood, I do,' said the big man.

'What could *Masters* possibly know about the Tipster?' inquired Lydia.

'Whatever it was, Miss Kenwood,' said Gordon, 'it was sufficiently important for the Tipster, not only to murder Masters, but to try and kill my wife and me, in case Masters should have given me a hint of what he knew when he rang me up. He fired five shots at us, but luckily only smashed the screen and a window of my car.'

'This morning?' said Lydia, quickly. 'Where?'

'On the way to the *Compasses*,' said Vicky.

Iris gave a little exclamation.

'But that means he — he's in this district?' she said.

'It means 'e *was*,' remarked Mr. Budd. 'What d'you know about Maurice Swayne, Mr. Kenwood?'

'Swayne?' Kenwood repeated the name and Gordon thought it was to gain time to think out his reply. 'He's gone . . . back to London . . . '

'Left this mornin', I 'ear,' said Mr. Budd. 'D'yer know his address?'

'No,' said Kenwood. 'No, I'm afraid I don't . . . '

'I understand 'e was a friend of yours?'

'I know very little about him as a matter of fact.' Kenwood looked uncomfortable. Quite clearly the subject was one he did not like.

'What I don't understand,' broke in Iris

Latimer, suddenly, 'is how *could* Masters have found out anything about the Tipster?'

'We shan't know that, Miss Latimer,' said Gordon, 'until we learn *who* the Tipster is.'

'*I* think the man is a maniac,' said Lydia, shrugging her shoulders. 'No sane person would go about murdering people for no earthly reason.'

Gordon looked at her. He said: 'Perhaps the Tipster has a very good reason, Miss Kenwood.'

'It's all horrible . . . horrible . . . ' muttered Iris. Her face was white and strained. In her large eyes was a look that puzzled Gordon. It was a mixture of fear and perplexity combined with some other emotion that he could not place. It was only natural, he supposed, that she should be upset . . . but was it the brutal murder of Masters that caused it?

'You can't call this murder the act of a *sane* man, Cross,' remarked David Kenwood. 'There was no need to batter his face and head so savagely . . . '

'I agree — that looks like sheer wanton

160

ferocity,' said Gordon. 'The act of a man in a paroxysm of rage . . . '

'It was beastly . . . perfectly beastly,' said Vicky, with a shiver.

Mr. Budd yawned.

'Sane or insane,' he said, heavily, 'we've got ter find 'im, an' put a stop to these killin's . . . ' He hoisted himself on to his feet. 'I must be gettin' back ter London . . . Are you comin', Mr. Cross?'

'Yes,' said Gordon, and then suddenly: 'Oh — by the way, Miss Latimer. There was a friend of yours in the *Compasses* this morning . . . '

She looked at him with a flicker of uneasiness.

'Who . . . who do you mean?' she asked.

'The man you were with last night — at the Odds On club,' he answered.

'Oh . . . yes . . . was he?' she remarked nervously.

'*Did* you go to the Odds On last night?' asked Lydia.

'Only for a minute — to . . . to see a friend of daddy's . . . '

'Who was that, Iris?' asked Kenwood curiously.

She looked confused. A soft colour came into her pale cheeks.

'You . . . wouldn't know him, David,' she said. 'I . . . '

A knock at the door interrupted her and she stopped in evident relief at the interruption. The maid came in carrying a salver.

'Excuse me, miss,' said the girl. 'This letter is for you.'

'Letter?' Iris frowned at the envelope on the tray. 'But there's no post until . . . '

'It didn't come by post, miss,' explained the girl. 'I've just found it in the letter-box.'

'Thank you, Mary,' said Iris. She took the letter and the maid went out. Still frowning, Iris muttered an apology and slit open the envelope.

'Oh!' she exclaimed, as she glanced at the contents.

'What is it?' asked David Kenwood quickly.

'Read it,' she said faintly. 'It's . . . it's from the Tipster . . . '

Kenwood almost snatched it from her fingers.

'*I regret that I was forced to eliminate Masters,*' he read aloud. '*It was, unfortunately, a necessity. He knew too much. The Tipster.*'

'Let me 'ave that, please, sir,' said Mr. Budd.

'Just a minute,' Kenwood stared at the type-written note in surprise. 'I know the machine on which this was typed . . . '

'You do, Mr. Kenwood,' said Mr. Budd.

'Yes . . . I'm sure of it,' Kenwood nodded quickly. 'Look, the capital 'I' is out of alignment and there's no tail to the 'y' . . . '

'The same characteristics as the note we found in Crawford's pocket . . . ' put in Gordon excitedly.

'What machine do *you* think this was typed on?' asked Mr. Budd.

'A Royal portable,' answered Kenwood, 'belonging to Maurice Swayne.'

III

Perched on the arm of the settee, Vicky turned the pages of the telephone directory, a frown of concentration on her pretty face.

'Can't you find it?' asked Gordon, lighting a cigarette and looking up from the depths of his armchair.

'Give me a chance,' she said. 'I've only just got to the S's . . . '

'Perhaps he hasn't got a telephone . . . '

'Don't keep on talking, Gordon,' she said, irritably. 'Stone, Strong, Street, Sudwort — what a *peculiar* name! — Swot . . . Here we are — Swayne, Maurice. River Dream, River bank, Staines — Staines 78190 . . . '

'River Dream?' Gordon got up and came over to her, peering down over her shoulder. 'That sounds like one of those bungalow places . . . '

'Or a house-boat, Gordon,' suggested Vicky. 'That's just the sort of place Swayne would choose to live in. He could do what he liked without much fear of being overlooked. I should think it's much more likely to be a house-boat . . . '

'Why?' asked Gordon.

'A house-boat is more isolated . . . '

'H'm . . . ' He nodded, thoughtfully.

'What was that number again, darling?'

'Staines 78190 . . . What are you going to do?'

'Ring up and see if there's any reply.' He walked over to the telephone and dialled Toll.

'Surely he wouldn't go back *there*,' said Vicky.

'He might — you never know,' said Gordon. 'Anyway, there may be somebody there . . . ' The operator's voice broke in demanding to know what number he wanted. 'Staines 78190, please,' said Gordon. 'This is Terminus 69421 . . . If there's no reply we can assume the place is empty.'

'What then?' she asked.

'We'll run up to Staines and go on a little tour of inspection,' he answered.

'I told you Swayne was the Tipster all along, didn't I?' she said complacently. Gordon grinned at her over the telephone.

'I don't remember you telling me anything of the kind,' he said.

'There must be something wrong with your memory, then,' she retorted.

'*My* recollection is that you were convinced it was *Masters*.'

'What nonsense!' she cried indignantly. 'You know perfectly well, Gordon Cross, that's not true . . . You're just being pig-headed . . . '

'There's no reply,' he broke in, and hung the receiver back on its rack.

'You didn't expect there would be, did you?' she demanded.

'No, but I wanted to make sure,' he said. 'Later on to-night, Vicky, we'll go and take a look at this place River Dream. It might be very interesting.'

It was half-past eleven when Gordon drove Vicky slowly along the towpath at Staines. The moon was shining from a cloudless sky and it was almost as bright as day. The river flowed with scarcely a ripple reflecting the light of the moon with mirror clearness.

'Hadn't you better *ask* somebody, Gordon?' suggested Vicky, after they had searched unsuccessfully for the place they were seeking.

Gordon surveyed the deserted stretch of river and towpath and the unsightly

166

gloomy bulk of the gas-works, which for some unknown reason had been built on the river bank.

'Who shall I ask, darling, out of this vast concord of people?' he asked, sarcastically.

'Don't be ridiculous,' said Vicky, crossly. 'I meant . . . '

'It must be somewhere about here,' he went on. 'We haven't passed it . . . '

'What do you expect to find there?' she asked.

'I don't know — perhaps nothing — perhaps a lot . . . '

'Look,' she broke in, 'there are some house-boats . . . over there against the opposite bank . . . '

'Can you make out the names?' he asked.

'Slow down a little,' she said, peering out the open side window. 'Camelot . . . Lazydays . . . Heart's Desire . . . '

'No good to us,' he said.

'There's another house-boat further along all by itself . . . '

'That sounds more promising,' he said. He increased the speed until they were opposite the solitary house-boat and then slowed again.

'That's it, Gordon,' exclaimed Vicky, excitedly. 'That's River Dream. I *was* right about its being a house-boat . . . '

He stopped the car and got out.

'Quite a big place, isn't it?' he said, as Vicky joined him on the towpath.

'Yes.' She stared dubiously across the smooth river. 'But how do we get across? There's a dinghy tied up to the house-boat, but nothing *this* side . . . '

'Forethought, darling — forethought,' he replied. 'I put on my swim suit underneath my clothes before we left home . . . '

'Why didn't you tell me?' she demanded. 'I could have done the same.'

'I never thought of it, darling . . . '

'So, what am I going to do?' said Vicky.

'I'm afraid you'll just have to stay here, Vicky,' he said.

'Oh, will I?' she retorted. 'We'll see about that. If you're going to swim across so am I . . . '

She began to unbutton her blouse.

'Vicky . . . ' cried Gordon. 'You can't . . . '

'You just try and stop me, Gordon Cross,' she said.

'But you . . . Vicky, keep your clothes on!'

'Don't be silly,' she answered, loosening her skirt. 'There's nobody to see me — and my undies are quite respectable. No worse than a swim suit anyhow . . . Oh, look . . . look, there's somebody in the house-boat after all. I saw a light — like the flicker of a torch . . . '

Gordon swung round. The dark shadows of the house-boat's cabin lit up faintly — intermittent flashes as though someone were searching with a torch.

'You're right,' he said. 'I'm going over . . . '

He began to undress rapidly.

'You wait for me,' said Vicky. 'I'm coming with you . . . '

She slipped out of her skirt and took off her blouse.

'Who do you think it is over there?' she whispered, as she stooped to pull off her shoes. 'Swayne?'

'I shouldn't think so,' said Gordon. 'He wouldn't bother to move about with a torch, would he?'

He kicked off his shoes.

169

'How long are you going to be?'

'I'm ready now,' she said.

'Come on then,' he said and slid down the bank into the river with scarcely a splash. Vicky followed him, a slim attractive figure in her flimsy underwear.

'Don't make a noise,' he whispered. 'Swim as quietly as you can . . . We don't want to scare whoever it is . . . '

'All right,' she said. 'Come on . . . '

They swam silently side by side. The water was warm and they made scarcely a sound.

'Are we — nearly — there?' asked Vicky, breathlessly, when they had been swimming for what seemed to her a long time.

'Not . . . much further . . . now . . . ' gasped Gordon. 'It's further . . . than . . . it looks . . . '

They reached the house-boat at last and clung on to the landing stage.

'Hang on, Vicky,' whispered Gordon. 'I'll pull myself out first . . . ' He hauled himself up, dripping, on to the deck.

'Give me your hand,' he muttered.

She did so, and he pulled her out of the water.

'Look,' he said, under his breath, when she stood beside him. 'There's a door there . . . Come on — quietly . . . '

They tiptoed over to the door of the cabin, their bare feet scarcely making a sound. Gordon tried the handle and found that the door was unlocked. He opened it a few inches.

'Listen,' he said, with his lips close to Vicky's ear. 'There's somebody inside . . . '

She nodded. She could hear the sound of movements inside, the rustle of papers and the noise of drawers being opened and closed.

'Who do you think it is?' she whispered.

'I don't know,' he answered, 'it's too dark inside to see. I'm going in . . . '

'Be careful,' breathed Vicky, urgently.

He threw open the door with a crash and there was a half-stifled scream. He caught somebody by the arm and called to Vicky: 'Pull back the curtains at the windows . . . '

She did so and bright moonlight flooded the cabin of the house-boat. Gordon looked at his struggling captive and uttered a surprised ejaculation.

'Miss Kenwood! You!'

'Please let go of my arm, Mr. Cross,' she said, breathlessly. 'You . . . you're hurting me . . . '

'What are you doing here?' demanded Vicky.

'I . . . came to see . . . to see Mr. Swayne,' said Lydia. She was recovering her usual coolness.

'Did you expect to find him in one of the drawers of that desk, Miss Kenwood?' asked Gordon, nodding towards a large desk, all the drawers of which had been pulled out.

'You've no right to question me,' she said defiantly.

'You were looking for something, weren't you?' he said.

'That's my business,' she retorted.

'Not in the circumstances,' he said, and stopped abruptly.

Slow and heavy footsteps sounded on the deck outside.

'There's somebody out there,' whispered Vicky.

The footsteps drew nearer to the door and they all three waited expectantly. And then a voice said: 'Whoever yer are in there, yer'd better come out . . . an' don't make no trouble 'cos I've got several men within call . . . '

'Budd!' cried Gordon, in relief.

The huge figure of Mr. Budd loomed in the doorway.

'Mr. Cross,' he said, 'I didn't expect to find *you* 'ere. Who've yer got with yer?'

'My wife and Miss Kenwood.'

'Miss Kenwood?' grunted the big man, in surprise. 'Did she come with you?'

'No,' said Vicky, 'we found her here.'

Mr. Budd came further into the cabin. He looked around him and then at Lydia Kenwood, rubbing at his fleshy chin.

'Thought you didn't know Swayne's address, Miss Kenwood?' he remarked, sleepily.

'*I* never said I didn't,' she answered calmly. 'Aren't you confusing me with my brother?'

'How did *you* get here, Budd?' asked Gordon, curiously.

'Been keepin' a watch on the place ever since we found out it belonged to Swayne,' said Mr. Budd — 'from the island there . . . ' He jerked his head towards the deck. ' 'Ad an idea somebody might turn up sooner or later. Got Leek an' a coupla men on the job. What brought you 'ere, Miss Kenwood?'

'It's pretty obvious, isn't it?' said Vicky. 'Look at the place . . . '

Mr. Budd surveyed the disordered cabin. Drawers had been pulled out and papers lay scattered all over the place.

'Did you do all this, Miss Kenwood?' he said. 'H'm . . . You seem to have turned everythin' pretty well upside down. What were you lookin' for?'

'I don't have to answer that,' she said.

Mr. Budd sighed gently.

'Well, I can't make you,' he said. 'But I think, maybe, you'd be wiser if you did . . . '

'Is that a threat?' she demanded.

'No, miss,' he answered. 'Just a bit o' sensible advice . . . You came over in the boat, didn't you?'

'Yes,' she said, shortly.

'We swam across,' began Vicky.

'Yes, Mrs. Cross.' He looked at her scanty attire, and suddenly remembering what she had on she snatched the cloth off the table and wrapped it round her. 'Well, I think you'd best all go back in the boat with me,' went on Mr. Budd, 'an' we'll go an' 'ave a little talk somewhere. I don't want a lot o' people 'angin' about this place for a bit . . . '

'You think Swayne may come here?' put in Gordon.

'Maybe . . . ' said Mr. Budd. 'Now let's get goin', shall we? You can keep that table cloth you've got wrapped round you, Mrs. Cross. It looks very becomin' . . . '

'Thank you,' said Vicky, sweetly.

They went out on to the deck.

'You'd better get into the boat first, Budd,' said Gordon. 'I'll untie her and get in last . . . '

'Right you are, Mr. Cross,' agreed the big man. ' 'Old her steady, will yer?'

Gordon complied and Mr. Budd got down gingerly into the swaying dinghy. Vicky and Lydia followed him and Gordon untied the rope from the iron ring. He jumped into the boat, took one of the oars and pushed off.

'Nice night for a bit o' boatin','

remarked Mr. Budd, as Gordon began to row towards the opposite bank. 'Moonlight an' not a cloud in the sky . . . '

'Have you got anybody watching from the bank, Mr. Budd?' asked Vicky, suddenly.

He shook his head.

'No, Mrs. Cross,' he answered. 'My men are on the island be'ind the 'ouse-boat . . . '

'Then who's that man by the car, Gordon?' she demanded.

'Somebody taking a stroll,' he suggested, and Mr. Budd twisted his huge back round so that he could see the towpath.

'He's got something in his hand,' began Vicky.

Mr. Budd saw the glint in the moonlight and some instinct warned him.

'Get down flat — all of you!' he cried, sharply, and he had scarcely spoken when a spurt of flame came from the man on the bank and a bullet whined over their heads. It struck the water with a 'phut' and a splash. The shot was followed by another, and another. A bullet struck the blade of one of the oars.

'Keep down,' muttered Mr. Budd. 'He hasn't gone yet . . . '

Several more shots whistled round the boat and then silence.

Gordon raised his head cautiously and looked over the gunwale.

'It's all right now, I think,' he said. 'He's going away . . . '

'Lucky I saw the moon glint on 'is gun,' grunted Mr. Budd.

'Who was it?' asked Lydia.

As if in answer to her question somebody began to whistle softly. The melody of Debussy's 'Clair de Lune' came floating towards them over the silent running river.

Vicky caught her breath.

'Gordon,' she whispered. 'It was the Tipster.'

8

I

Gordon Cross woke up to the sound of his wife's voice calling to him: 'Gordon,' it said, sleepily. 'Gordon . . . Wake up!'

He rolled over in bed, and, without opening his eyes inquired irritably what the trouble was about.

'Wake up,' persisted Vicky. 'The telephone's ringing . . . '

'Well, why don't you answer it?' he demanded and sat up, yawning. 'Lord . . . I'm tired . . . '

'It's stopped now,' said Vicky. 'How about a cup of tea, Gordon?'

'Jolly good idea,' he said, snuggling down again into the pillow.

'Suppose you get up and make some?' she suggested.

He groaned.

'I thought you meant *you* were getting up,' he said.

178

'Don't be lazy,' she began severely, and then the telephone bell started again.

'Damn . . . there's the phone again,' he grunted unnecessarily.

'You'd better see who it is,' she said. 'It may be important.'

He got out of bed grumbling and rubbing his head. Still only half awake he stumbled into the sitting-room and picked up the receiver.

'Hello?' he called.

The voice of Jacob Bellamy came out of the ear-piece.

'Good mornin', cock,' he greeted cheerfully. 'Ain't it a grand mornin', eh?'

'What's the matter with you, Jacob?' demanded Gordon. 'Night starvation?'

'Wotcher mean, boy?' asked the old man in surprise.

'Ringing up at this hour . . . ' grunted Gordon.

'Got yer out o' bed, did I?' said Bellamy. 'He chuckled. 'Blimey! It's 'alf-past eight, cock . . . Listen! I think I got some news for yer — about you-know-what.'

'The Tipster?' asked Gordon eagerly.

'No names, no pack drill, boy,' said

Jacob. 'What about you an' the missus poppin' into the club ter-night, eh? Round about nine . . . Got ter be out o' town all day . . . '

'Right you are, Jacob,' agreed Gordon. 'You've *really* got something?'

'Tell yer all about it when I see yer, cock,' said Jacob Bellamy. 'Now yer can go back ter bed . . . '

'What time did *you* get up?' asked Gordon.

A throaty chuckle rumbled in his ear.

'I *ain't* up, boy,' he said. 'Got the phone beside me bed. So long, cock. See yer ter-night . . . '

Gordon hung up and went back to the bedroom. Vicky had snuggled down again and was half asleep. She opened one eye and looked over the eiderdown drowsily.

'Who was it?' she asked.

'Jacob,' he answered. 'He's got some news. Wants us to go and see him at the club to-night . . . '

'About the Tipster?' she said.

'He wouldn't say over the phone, but I gather that's what he means,' said Gordon, brushing his hair. 'Cautious old devil, Jacob . . . '

Vicky sat up in bed, pushing the hair out of her eyes.

'I say, Gordon,' she said, blinking at him, 'the Tipster hasn't done anything about Mr. Tidmann, has he?'

'Not yet!' he replied.

'I don't see how he can,' she said. 'Not with two detectives guarding him day and night . . . '

'That didn't stop him getting Dukes, did it?'

'No, but this time it's different, isn't it?' she said. 'They're not letting Tidmann out of their sight for a moment.'

Gordon put down his brushes and examined his face in the mirror.

'I'll admit it seems impossible,' he said, gently rasping his chin with an exploring forefinger, 'but I wouldn't like to bet on Tidmann's chances . . . Are you getting up?'

'After you've brought me that cup of tea, darling,' she retorted. 'What are we doing to-day?'

'Well . . . ' He turned round and reached for his dressing-gown. 'I thought of going to Brighton races . . . '

'Why?' she asked.

'Don't you want to?'

'It 'ud be lovely, but why are we going?'

'Well — why does one *usually* go to the races?' he inquired.

'You've got some other reason than *that*,' she said.

'Perhaps I have,' he admitted.

'What is it?'

'I'm curious, Vicky — very curious. Budd told us last night that Mr. Lewis Tidmann will be there and I'm curious to see whether anything will happen to him — in spite of his bodyguard.'

II

'High Jinks'll do it, Gordon!' cried Vicky excitedly. 'High Jinks . . . High Jinks has won it! Gordon — that's twelve pounds I get . . . '

'So do I,' said Gordon. 'That's a good start for the day anyhow. You stay here, Vicky, and I'll go and collect our money.'

He left her on the stand and mingled

with the crowd. It was a lovely day and Brighton race-course lay baking under a blazing sun. The long spell of hot weather had made the going hard, and some of the results looked, in consequence, like being surprising.

'Hello, cock!' cried a hoarse voice, as Gordon forced his way through the crowd, and looking round he saw Jacob Bellamy pushing his way towards him.

'Hello, Jacob,' said Gordon. 'Didn't expect to see you. Did you back the winner?'

'Betcher life I did, boy,' grinned Bellamy.

'So did we . . . I say, what have you got hold of — about the Tipster?'

Jacob Bellamy gave him a warning look.

'Wait till ter-night, cock,' he said. 'I ain't goin' ter talk 'ere . . . '

'All right,' said Gordon. 'But you might give me some sort of hint . . . '

'I'll tell yer one thing, boy,' said the old man. 'Give yer somethin' ter chew on. Ever 'eard of Martin Carrington?'

'Martin Carrington?' Gordon shook his head. 'No . . . '

'Didn't think you would've,' Bellamy

chuckled. 'But you *will* . . . '

'Who is he?' demanded Gordon.

' 'E ain't anybody, cock — but I'll bet 'e was responsible for the Tipster.' Old Jacob patted him on the arm. 'See yer later, boy — put yer shirt on Apple Chutney in the next race — yer'll win a packet . . . '

He waved his hand and went off in the direction of the paddock. Gordon collected the money he and Vicky had won and made his way back to the stand.

'Here you are, darling,' he said, handing her a thin packet of notes. 'Twelve quid . . . '

'Thanks — was that Mr. Bellamy you were talking to?'

'Yes — being very mysterious about somebody called Martin Carrington who, apparently, doesn't exist . . . '

'I don't understand . . . ' She frowned.

'Neither do I,' said Gordon. 'I expect we shall hear all about it to-night. He gave me a tip for the next race — Apple Chutney. He says it's a certainty — I've put a fiver on at sevens . . . '

'Didn't you put anything on for me?' demanded Vicky, and when he shook his head: 'Well, I do think that's mean of you, Gordon Cross . . . I'm talking to you . . . '

'I say, Vicky,' he ignored her last remark, 'there's Kenwood — with his sister and Iris Latimer . . . '

'Where?' she asked. 'Oh, I see . . . '

'They're talking to Tidmann . . . '

'Is *that* Mr. Tidmann?' said Vicky, looking at the figure of the bookmaker disapprovingly. 'Well, I can't say I like the look of him very much.'

'Nasty piece of work,' agreed Gordon. 'Those two men next to him are the bodyguard, I suppose. Let's stroll over that way, Vicky . . . '

'What about my money on Apple Chutney?' she demanded.

'How much do you want to put on?'

'The same as you, of course.'

He held out his hand.

'Hand it over then, darling,' he said.

She gave him five pounds of her winnings.

'You go over to the Kenwoods,' he said. 'I'll go and put this on and join you . . . '

She made her way slowly towards the little group, timing herself so that she should not get there before Gordon returned. The result was that they both got there together.

'Good afternoon, Mr. Tidmann,' said Gordon.

The bookmaker looked round.

'Oh, 'ullo, Mr. Cross,' he said. ' 'Avin' a day at the races, eh? You know Miss Latimer an' . . . ?'

'We all know each other, don't we, Mr. Gross?' broke in Lydia Kenwood. 'I do hope you two didn't catch a cold last night, Mrs. Cross?'

'We didn't catch *anything*, Miss Kenwood,' said Vicky, sweetly.

Iris Latimer looked from one to the other in a puzzled way.

'What *are* you talking about, Lydia?' she asked.

Lydia laughed.

'Nothing, Iris,' she said lightly. 'Just nonsense, that's all . . . '

'Well, you see, Cross,' remarked Tidmann jovially, 'in spite of the Tipster's threat I'm still alive an' well, eh?'

'I hope you will continue to remain so,' said Gordon.

'Of course I shall.' The bookmaker snapped his fingers. 'What can 'e do with these two fellers lookin' after me all the time? I can't even 'ave a bath on me own.'

He chuckled, but Kenwood looked serious.

'He's already killed four people, you know, Tidmann,' he said, 'and got away with it . . . '

'Well, I'm not goin' ter make the fifth,' declared Mr. Tidmann. 'This crazy lunatic 'as bitten off more'n he can chew with me.'

'That remains to be seen,' said Gordon, and then on a sudden impulse he added: 'By the way, have any of you ever heard of — Martin Carrington?'

Lewis Tidmann uttered an exclamation. His face went suddenly grey.

'Martin Carrington?' he repeated, hoarsely.

'What's the matter, Mr. Tidmann?' asked Vicky. 'Are you feeling ill?'

'No . . . no, I'm all right,' answered the bookmaker. 'It's . . . it's only . . . '

'Just another twinge of rheumatism, eh, Mr. Tidmann?' remarked Gordon.

III

'Do you know, Gordon,' said Vicky, when they had returned to the stand just before the race, 'if Mr. Bellamy's tip comes off we shall win seventy pounds between us?'

'Yes,' said Gordon. 'His other tip came off, didn't it?'

She looked puzzled.

'His *other* tip?' she said, questioningly.

'Martin Carrington,' he said.

'What is all this about Martin Carrington?' she demanded.

'I don't know — but Tidmann does, Vicky. He nearly had a fit when I mentioned the name . . . '

'What made you do it?'

'I rather wanted to see what effect it would have . . . '

The starting bell went and there was a roar from the crowd. Vicky, forgetting all about the mysterious Martin Carrington in her excitement, concentrated her attention on the bunch of horses that was sweeping towards them over the green turf.

'Here they come,' said Gordon. 'I can't

see Apple Chutney. They're all bunched together at the moment . . . '

'There's a horse coming out in front,' cried Vicky. 'Which is it?'

'It's not Apple Chutney . . . I think . . . Yes, it's the favourite — Sky Sign. There's Apple Chutney now! . . . Just coming out of the ruck . . . '

A wave of excitement spread over the watching crowd. There were shouts of 'Sky Sign . . . Sky Sign,' intermingled with a few enthusiasts for Apple Chutney.

'Sky Sign's keeping the lead,' said Vicky, standing almost on tiptoe so that she could see over the heads of the people in front of her. 'Why doesn't Apple Chutney come on?'

'I don't think Apple Chutney's going to make it,' said Gordon, anxiously. 'There's only a furlong to go . . . It's Sky Sign's race — Sky Sign's going to win it . . . No, by Jove, he isn't . . . '

His words were drowned by a mighty shout of 'Apple Chutney — Apple Chutney!' The horse — a big bay — suddenly streaked forward, leaving the rest behind him.

'Apple Chutney's done it,' said Gordon. 'Apple Chutney's done it . . . '

'We've won . . . Gordon, we've won!' Vicky clapped her hands.

'It was a wonderful race . . . ' began Gordon, and then above the chatter of the crowd came a woman's scream.

'What was that?' said Gordon.

'Somebody screamed — over there,' said Vicky. 'Gordon, something's happened . . . there's a crowd gathering . . . look . . . '

He forced his way through the crowd, with Vicky close behind him. Near the stand a large group of people had gathered and was getting momentarily larger. In the midst of them a policeman's helmet bobbed about like a little boat in a rough sea.

'What's happened?' Gordon elbowed his way into the crowd. 'Let me through here, will you?'

'Now then, now then — keep back there,' said the constable. 'Keep back there, please . . . '

Gordon caught sight of David Kenwood and called to attract his attention.

'Mr. Kenwood . . . Mr. Kenwood

. . . What's happened?'

'It's Tidmann, Cross.' David Kenwood's face was white and his voice shook. 'We were all watching the race . . . He gave a little choked cry and suddenly collapsed . . . '

'He's dead,' muttered Lydia.

'Who screamed?' asked Vicky.

'Iris,' answered Kenwood. 'She saw the blood . . . '

'Blood?' echoed Gordon, sharply.

'Somebody stabbed him — in the back,' said Lydia, and added with a little horrified cry: 'David . . . there's blood all over your hands.'

IV

Mr. Budd, looking very glum, sat in front of the big desk in the Assistant Commissioner's office. Colonel Blair, dapper as usual, but with an irritable frown on his face, eyed him sternly and rolled a pencil up and down his blotting pad.

'You realize why I've sent for you, Superintendent?' he remarked, coldly.

191

'Yes, sir,' said the big man.

'The murder of Tidmann,' said Colonel Blair, 'is the fifth crime perpetrated by this man, who calls himself the Tipster, within a fortnight. In four of these cases he gave a previous notice of his intention. In spite of this, however, you have been unable to afford these people adequate protection and the threats of this man have been successfully carried out. It's bad, Superintendent, and you know it's bad . . .'

'Yes sir, I'm afraid it looks like it,' murmured Mr. Budd.

'In the circumstances,' continued the Assistant Commissioner, 'you must realize there is only one course of action that I can take. I am loath to do it, considering your record, but in the public interest it's my duty. I shall have to take you off the case and give it to another officer. This man has *got* to be found before he commits any further outrages.'

Mr. Budd sighed.

'I understand, sir,' he said, slowly, 'but I should be very grateful if you'd give me another week before you do anythin' . . .'

Colonel Blair shook his sleek grey head.

'I'm afraid that's impossible, Budd,' he said. 'Unless, of course, you can offer some exceptionally good reason . . . '

'Well, sir, I think I can do that,' said Mr. Budd. He drew a deep breath and leaned forward. 'You see, I *know* who the Tipster is . . . '

'*What's* that?' Colonel Blair nearly jumped out of his chair. '*What* did you say?'

'I said, sir,' remarked Mr. Budd ponderously, 'I know who the Tipster is . . . '

'Then,' exploded the Assistant Commissioner, 'why the devil don't you arrest him?'

'It's not quite as easy as all that, sir,' said Mr. Budd. 'May I explain what I mean?'

'Yes, yes, of course,' said Colonel Blair impatiently.

'Well, then, sir, it's like this,' said Mr. Budd. He leaned forward and rested his arm on the desk. 'When I first took over this case after the murder o' Lord

Latimer . . . ' He talked for a quarter of an hour and the Assistant Commissioner listened intently. ' . . . And that's all it's possible to do at the moment, sir,' the big man concluded. 'We can't 'urry matters. If I act too 'astily the Tipster may easily slip through our fingers for good.'

'Yes, yes, I see the difficulty,' Colonel Blair nodded, quickly. 'I withdraw what I said previously, Superintendent. You can have another week — or longer if you require it. I'll give you a free hand . . . '

'Thank you, sir,' said the grateful Mr. Budd. 'I can promise you, you won't be without results for long.'

V

Gordon Cross and Vicky arrived at the Odds On just after nine and were greeted by Francaire, the head waiter.

'Mr. Bellamy ees expecting you,' he said. 'He wish you to go to ees office . . . Henri.' He called to one of the waiters. 'Take madame and m'sieu to Mr. Bellamy's office.'

'Oui, m'sieu,' said Henri. 'You come this way, please?'

They followed him through an arched doorway and up a flight of thickly carpeted stairs. At the end of a corridor, Henri knocked on a closed door.

'Come in,' called the voice of Jacob Bellamy.

The old man looked up from behind a huge desk as they entered.

''Ullo, boy . . . 'ullo, m'dear,' he said. 'Yer lookin' very nice . . . '

'Thank you,' said Vicky.

'Sit down, both of yer,' said Jacob, getting up and going over to a sideboard full of bottles and glasses 'What about a nice drop o' Scotch, eh? The real stuff, cock — none of yer hooch.'

He held up a bottle of John Haig.

'Ah . . . ' said Gordon. 'Yes — I think so, Jacob.'

Bellamy poured out three stiff pegs.

'Soda for me, please,' said Vicky.

The old man made a grimace.

'Spoilin' good stuff — that's what it is,' he said. 'There's only one way to drink good whisky an' that's straight.' He brought over the glasses. 'Whatcher think of this afternoon, eh?'

'You mean — Tidmann?' asked Gordon.

''Course I mean Tidmann, boy.' Bellamy drank some whisky. 'Clever, eh? The Tipster chose the one moment when everybody's attention 'ud be on somethin' else — includin' those perlice guards — the finish of a race. Smart, yer know. You've gotter 'and it to 'im, cock.'

'He took a risk . . . ' said Vicky.

'Not such a risk as you'd think,' remarked Gordon. 'It would be all over in a matter of seconds . . . Jacob, who is Martin Carrington?'

Jacob Bellamy chuckled.

'Ah, boy,' he said, 'we're comin' ter 'im. Martin Carrington's the 'ub o' the whole thing — or I'm a blue-nosed monkey . . . '

'I mentioned the name to Tidmann and it gave him a pretty bad shock,' said Gordon.

'I bet it did,' said the old man. 'I bet it did, cock.'

'Stop being mysterious, Mr. Bellamy,' said Vicky, 'and tell us what it means.'

'That's what I asked yer to come 'ere for.' Bellamy finished the rest of his whisky. 'You wanted ter find somethin' that connected all these people — Latimer, Crawford, Dukes, an' now Tidmann, didn't you?'

Gordon nodded.

'Well, Martin Carrington's the connection between 'em.'

'How,' asked Vicky. 'Who is he?'

''E ain't anybody, m' dear. 'E's bin dead for fifteen years . . . 'Ave another Haig, cock?'

'No, thanks,' said Gordon. 'Come to the point, Jacob. How is this man, who's been dead for fifteen years, connected with these four people?'

Bellamy poured himself out another drink — sipped it and smacked his lips.

'I'll tell you,' he said. 'Martin Carrington was a pretty well-known owner of race-'orses years ago. But 'e got in trouble. 'E was 'auled up before the stewards o' the Jockey Club at Newmarket an' accused of 'not tryin'' with one of his 'orses. 'E denied it, but the evidence was too strong an' 'e was warned off Newmarket 'eath an' all courses under the jurisdiction of the Jockey Club. That's 'ow they put it in the *Racin' Calendar*. I've got the actual copy 'ere. 'E couldn't face the disgrace an' shot 'imself . . . '

'But *what* has this got to do with . . . ' began Gordon.

'Don't you get impatient, cock,' went on Bellamy. 'You'll see in a minute. Lord Latimer was one o' the stewards — the others are dead — who conducted the inquiry. Crawford was the trainer o' the 'orse all the trouble was about. Dukes was the jockey what rode it, an' Tidmann was the bookmaker who *denied* that Carrington had backed the 'orse to win over twelve thousand quid, when Carrington called 'im as a witness in 'is favour. There was also a stable lad named George Murdoch who stated 'e'd over'eard Carrington instruct Dukes an' Crawford to give the 'orse an 'easy race' an' if necessary 'pull 'im' — confirming what they said themselves . . . '

'Jacob,' broke in Gordon excitedly, 'I believe we're getting somewhere . . . '

'I ain't finished yet, boy,' said Mr. Bellamy, complacently. 'The name of the 'orse was — Clair de Lune.'

'That clinches it,' said Gordon. 'I knew that tune was important.'

'But,' remarked Vicky, frowning, 'how does the Tipster come into it?'

'Don't you see,' said Gordon, 'we've got a motive at last — a real, practical, concrete motive. Somebody's getting back on all the people who were responsible for Carrington's disgrace and subsequent suicide . . . Jacob, I suppose you remember the whole thing well?'

'You betcher life I do, cock . . . '

'Then tell me — do you think that Carrington was guilty?'

'No, I never did,' declared the old man. 'I allus thought it was a put-up job what Crawford, Dukes an' Tidmann 'ad 'atched up between 'em . . . '

'And this stable lad — Murdoch?'

'I think they just paid 'im well ter say what 'e did . . . '

'Why?' asked Vicky. 'Why did they want to injure Carrington?'

Bellamy shook his head.

'I can't tell you *that*, m' dear,' he said. 'But I allus thought that's what it was.

An' I'll bet it was Tidmann's scheme . . . '

'Yes . . . yes, no wonder it gave him a shock when I mentioned Carrington's name and told him about the Tipster whistling 'Clair de Lune',' said Gordon.

'Then the Tipster,' said Vicky, 'if he's killing these people for what they did to Carrington, must be somebody who was closely related to . . . '

'Had Carrington any family, Jacob?' asked Gordon.

'He was a widower,' answered Bellamy, 'but 'e 'ad a son an' a daughter — the gel was seven — the boy nearly fifteen . . . '

'That'd make them twenty-two and thirty now, wouldn't it?' remarked Gordon.

'What happened to them?' asked Vicky, 'after Carrington's death?'

'The little gel was adopted,' said old Jacob slowly. 'The boy was sent to a cousin o' Carrington's in Canada . . . '

'What happened to him after that?' inquired Gordon.

'I don't know, cock,' answered the bookmaker. 'But if 'e's alive, an' 'e ain't still in Canada, then I think . . . '

'We've found the Tipster?' ended

Gordon, as he paused.

Bellamy nodded.

'Who adopted the little girl?' said Vicky. 'Where is she now?'

'You've met 'er, m'dear,' answered Bellamy unexpectedly.

'We have?' exclaimed Gordon. 'Who is she?'

Jacob Bellamy looked from one to the other of them before he replied.

'Iris Latimer,' he said.

9

I

Gordon Cross nearly dropped his empty glass.

'Iris Latimer?' he repeated incredulously.

'Are you *sure*, Mr. Bellamy?' said Vicky.

''Course I'm sure, m'dear,' said the old man. 'Old Jacob Bellamy don't make them sort o' mistakes. Latimer was a good 'earted chap. 'E was a friend o' Carrington's and although 'e 'ad to do 'is duty over the runnin' of Clair de Lune, the thought of the little gel worried 'im. He was childless himself an' his wife 'ad died the year before. The adoption was all legal an' above board . . .'

Gordon got up and began to walk up and down the room.

'Don't you see what this means?' he said. 'It gives *Iris Latimer* a motive for . . .'

'You're not suggesting that she is the Tipster, are you, Gordon?' said Vicky.

'If you are, cock, yer crackers,' declared Bellamy.

'Why?' demanded Gordon.

'Because it's ridiculous,' said Vicky. 'The Tipster's a man . . . '

'Would you be prepared to swear to that, Vicky?' said Gordon.

'Well, I . . . I suppose . . . ' She stopped, looking a little disconcerted.

'You wouldn't,' said Gordon. 'That queer voice of his is the only thing you have to go on. And a woman could *assume* that easily. There's nothing the Tipster has done that a *woman* couldn't have done . . . '

'What about Dukes?' said Vicky. 'Getting his body down his fire-escape and up ours . . . '

'Dukes was a jockey,' said Gordon. 'He was small and weighed very little. An athletic woman like Iris Latimer could have done it easily. And don't forget the handkerchief I found by Crawford's body . . . '

'Sounds a bit far fetched ter me, cock,'

commented Bellamy.

'I think it's more likely to be the son,' said Vicky. 'You don't know where he is now, Mr. Bellamy?'

'Not an idea,' answered Bellamy. 'The last I 'eard of 'im was that 'e'd gone to Canada — like I told yer . . . '

'I'm sure he isn't there now,' said Vicky. 'He'd be thirty, wouldn't he? About the same age as — Maurice Swayne . . . '

'That slimy snake!' Bellamy's face flushed with anger. 'I can't imagine Carrington's son ever turnin' out like 'im . . . '

'A lot can happen in fifteen years, Mr. Bellamy . . . '

'It could quite easily be Swayne, you know,' said Gordon.

'*I* don't think there's any doubt about it,' declared Vicky.

'There don't seem ter be any doubt that 'e killed that poor feller, Masters,' grunted Bellamy.

'No, there doesn't,' said Gordon. 'Still we mustn't take it for granted, you know. We've got to try and trace Carrington's son, Jacob. What was his name?'

Bellamy's brows contracted.

'Now just a sec., cock,' he said. 'What *was* 'is name? . . . 'Enry — that's it . . . 'Enry Carrington.'

'We've got to find him,' said Gordon. 'He and Iris Latimer are probably in this together. That would account for Masters, wouldn't it? Masters found out somehow about Iris Latimer . . . That's why he phoned me. That's why he was killed . . . It all fits, Vicky, it all fits . . . '

'I can't believe that Iris 'ud 'ave anythin' ter do with killin' old Latimer,' said Bellamy. 'After all 'e done for her . . . '

'Neither do I,' agreed Vicky. 'It's ridiculous.'

'Well, we shall see,' said Gordon. 'It's a pity that Tidmann's dead. We could have made him tell us all about this conspiracy that made Carrington shoot himself . . . By Jove!' He stopped. 'The stable lad!' he ejaculated.

'What *are* you talking about, darling?' asked Vicky.

'The stable lad — what's-his-name,' said Gordon. 'The fellow who said he'd heard Carrington give orders to Dukes and Crawford to 'pull' the horse?'

'Murdoch, you mean, cock?'

'That's the fellow. *He* knows about this business, doesn't he?' said Gordon. 'He was in it — where's he to be found now, Jacob?'

'Now yer askin' somethin', boy,' said Bellamy, scratching his head. 'I ain't 'eard o' George Murdoch in years . . . '

'It shouldn't be difficult to find him,' said Gordon. 'He must be still alive because — don't you see? — if we're right he's the next person the Tipster means to kill.'

II

A sluggish stream, green scummed and unpleasant-looking flowed from under a broken waterwheel whose blackened timbers blended with the dark water. By the side of the wheel stood a broken-down house, with sagging roof and broken windows. It was half-hidden by trees and the weeds grew thickly all round it. There was an unwholesome smell that hung in the air — a smell of rottenness.

Gordon Cross and Vicky stood by a broken gate and surveyed this dismal place without enthusiasm.

'Are you sure this is the right place, Gordon?' asked Vicky, doubtfully.

'Must be,' he answered. 'Look, there's the old mill stream that used to work the old wheel . . . this is the Mill House.'

'But the house,' she protested. 'It's all falling to pieces . . . nobody could possibly live there — surely?'

'Murdoch does. This was the address the registration people gave me. I'll admit it looks pretty grim — even in daylight. Come on, Vicky, let's go and see if it's as dismal inside . . . '

He opened the gate and it gave a loud and protesting squeak.

'A drop of oil'd do that good,' he said. 'Look at the hinges — red with rust. Murdoch doesn't seem to care much for his surroundings. Look at the place — almost waist high with weeds and nettles . . . better be careful of your legs, Vicky . . . '

They picked their way gingerly up to

the almost invisible path.

'Look,' said Vicky, suddenly. 'There's a man fishing over there, on the other side of the stream . . . I suppose it isn't Murdoch?'

'I don't know,' said Gordon. 'It might be. I've never seen Murdoch . . . We'll try the house first, anyway.'

They reached the paintless, blistered door under the remains of a porch, and knocked. The sound echoed hollowly within.

'It sounds empty, doesn't it?' he said.

Vicky nodded.

'I'm quite sure nobody lives here . . . they couldn't,' she said. 'It must be horribly damp . . . Can't you smell how dank the air is? Like rotting wood and vegetation . . . '

'That's probably what it is.' He knocked again. 'There doesn't seem to be anyone at home . . . '

'Let's go and ask the fisherman . . . '

'We'll try once more.' He knocked loudly and long and at last there came the sound of unsteady steps within.

'Here comes somebody,' he whispered.

There was the rattle of a bolt and the door opened an inch, creaking loudly.

'Wot d'yer want?' demanded a surly

voice, and a dirty face with unkempt hair appeared round the edge of the door.

'Mr. Murdoch?' inquired Gordon.

'Yes — that's me,' answered the hoarse voice. 'Wot d'yer want?'

'I'd like to have a little talk with you,' began Gordon.

'I don' want ter talk ter no one,' snarled Murdoch, rudely. 'Go 'way an' leave me alone . . . '

He attempted to shut the door but Gordon put his foot in the aperture.

'Just a minute,' he said. 'Do you remember Martin Carrington?'

The man gave a sudden gasp.

' 'Ere what's yer game?' he demanded, thickly. 'Who sent yer?'

'So you *do* remember Martin Carrington, eh?' said Gordon.

'No. Who is 'e?'

'It won't do, Murdoch,' said Gordon. 'You gave yourself away the first time . . . '

'I didn't give nuthin' away — and I ain't, see?' said Murdoch. 'You sheer off both of yer. I don't know yer an' I don't want ter . . . '

'My name is Cross — Gordon Cross.

This is my wife. I don't know whether you set any value on your life, Murdoch, but if you do you'd better drop that surly attitude and listen to what I've got to say . . .'

'What yer talkin' about?' demanded the man.

'I've no intention of talking at all out here,' said Gordon. 'Don't you think we might continue our conversation inside? There's less chance of being overheard.'

'There's no one to over'ear anythin' 'ere. But yer can come in if yer wants to.' Murdoch's voice was slightly less surly, and a frightened look came into his small red-lidded eyes. He held the door open and they entered. The place was appalling in its filth. The bare boards were encrusted with dirt and the plaster of the broken walls was thick with grime. It was incredible that any human being could live in such a place, but looking at Murdoch, Gordon decided that he blended very well with his surroundings. He was an uncouth man with matted hair and the ingrained filth of weeks. He had shed almost every human attribute and sunk to a state that was lower than the animal.

He led the way into a back room that contained a plain deal table, stained with the remains of countless meals, a chair, and a bed in one corner piled with dirty blankets, and obviously in the same state as when he had got out of it that morning.

'Now what is it yer want?' demanded Murdoch.

'I want to know the truth about Martin Carrington,' said Gordon.

'I don't know what the 'ell you're talkin' about . . . '

'Oh, yes, I think you do,' broke in Gordon, sternly. 'Fifteen years ago you were a witness against Martin Carrington at the Stewards' inquiry, which resulted in his being 'warned off' — and brought about his death . . . '

'Well, what if I was?' grunted Murdoch. 'What business is it of yours?'

'Why did you take part in this plot to ruin him?'

'Plot? There wasn't no plot . . . '

'Come now, Murdoch — that's not true. Lewis Tidmann tells another story . . . '

'Tidmann? 'Ave you come from Tidmann?' Murdoch's small eyes narrowed.

'What's 'e told you, eh?'

'Enough to get you into very serious trouble, unless you're sensible and tell the truth,' said Gordon.

'The double-crossin' swine!' snarled Murdoch. 'I only did as I was ordered. It was Tidmann's scheme — 'im an' Crawford's. They'd been dopin' 'orses an' they thought Carrington 'ad got on to it. Tidmann said if they could get 'im 'warned off' noby'ud believe anythin' he said about 'em . . . '

'I see,' Gordon nodded. 'Discredit the witness, eh?'

'Wotcher say?'

'Nothing — go on.'

'Well, that's all. They give me fifty quid an' told me what ter say, an' I said it . . . '

'And Carrington shot himself,' said Gordon, and his face was very hard. 'A swell little set up.'

'We didn't reckon on that,' said Murdoch.

'But I've no doubt you were all very much relieved. I'm not sure there isn't something to be said for the Tipster after all.'

'The Tipster?' repeated Murdoch. ' 'Oo's 'e?'

'Don't you read the newspapers?'

'No.'

'You must be the only person in England who's never heard of the Tipster, I should imagine,' said Gordon. 'Now listen to me very carefully, Murdoch, because your life may depend on your doing exactly what I tell . . . '

'Wotcher mean?' demanded Murdoch, with sudden alarm. 'All this 'appened years ago . . . What's the idea o' . . . '

'Don't interrupt — listen,' snapped Gordon curtly. 'At the moment you're quite safe, but from the time certain information reaches me you'll be in danger — the greatest danger you've probably been in in your life . . . '

' 'Ere — what are you . . . '

'It's true, Mr. Murdoch,' put in Vicky, quietly. 'Somebody is out to kill you for what you did to Mr. Carrington. They have already killed Crawford, Dukes, and Tidmann . . . '

'Tidmann?' Murdoch looked at Gordon. 'I thought you said . . . '

'Never mind what I said,' he interrupted. 'Tidmann is dead. He was murdered. Unless you want the same thing to happen to you, you'd better do as I tell you . . . '

'Who's this feller yer talkin' about — this Tipster?'

'He's the person you are in danger from.'

Murdoch looked uneasy.

'I don't know what yer game is,' he muttered, 'but . . . '

'It's no game, I can assure you,' said Gordon. 'It was very serious for those other people who were in this conspiracy with you and it'll be very serious for you if you don't do as you're told.'

'You really mean that this feller's out ter *kill* me?'

'That's what I'm trying to make you understand.'

'Strewth . . . ' Murdoch wiped the back of his hand across his lips. 'What can I do?'

'For the present, nothing,' said Gordon, 'except stay where you are. Don't leave this place for any length of time during the day and not at all after dark. Shut yourself up and don't let anybody in. You'll be seeing me again very soon and then I'll tell you the rest of it . . . '

'But look 'ere . . . '

'That's all now, Murdoch,' said Gordon. 'Don't forget unless you do exactly what I say — *exactly* mind — nothing can save your life. Come on, Vicky, let's go . . . '

' 'Ere, not so fast,' said Murdoch. 'Are you the p'lice?'

'No.'

' 'Ow am I ter know yer playin' straight?' said Murdoch, suspiciously. 'S'posin'?'

'You'll have to risk it, won't you?' answered Gordon curtly. 'Use your common-sense, man. Would we come all this way if we didn't want to save your life? Do what I tell you and you'll be all right . . . '

'All right — I will,' said Murdoch sullenly.

'That's sensible.'

'When'll yer be comin' again?'

'Very soon, I think. But you needn't worry. I'm sending a friend of mine in a few hours to look after you . . . '

' 'Ow'll I know 'e's from you?'

'See this ring,' Gordon held out his hand. 'He'll have it with him. Come along, Vicky.'

When they were once more outside Gordon breathed a sigh of relief.

'Uncouth brute, isn't he?' he remarked.

Vicky nodded.

'Who's coming to look after him?' she asked.

'Jacob Bellamy.'

'Have you asked him?'

'Not yet,' he said, 'but I know he'll do it. He's crazy for a spot of excitement, and I think he'll get all he wants before we're through.'

He opened the gate and held it for her. As she passed through she glanced across the stream.

'The fisherman's still there,' she said.

'Yes . . . You know, Vicky, he rather interests me . . . '

'You think he's not just an ordinary fisherman?'

'No. Of course it might be just a coincidence that he's chosen that particular spot, but I'm a little doubtful . . . '

'You mean — he's watching Murdoch?' she asked, quickly.

'Don't you think it looks rather like it?'

At that moment the fisherman turned

his head and she saw his face for the first time.

'Gordon,' she said. 'Do you see who it is?'

'Yes, I see,' he answered. 'I *was* right, Vicky. It's the man who came into the *Compasses* that day — the man whom Iris Latimer met at Bellamy's place the other night.'

III

Mr. Budd came into his office and threw his hat on a chair.

'Anythin' come in, Leek?' he inquired.

The lean sergeant shook his head.

'Nuthin' at all,' he answered lugubriously.

The big man sat down heavily behind his desk.

'Where the devil can 'e be 'idin' 'imself?' he grunted, irritably. 'With the p'lice o' the whole country lookin' for 'im, you wouldn't think it was too easy, would you?'

'It's queer, ain't it?' said Leek.

'H'm,' said Mr. Budd. 'Any message from Cross?'

'No.'

'I wonder what 'e's up to,' murmured Mr. Budd, staring sleepily at the inkpot. 'You've still got those fellers watchin' the 'ouse-boat?'

'Yes,' answered Leek. 'Personally I think it's a waste of time.'

'You think most thin's is a waste o' time.'

'Well, 'e ain't likely ter go back there, is 'e?'

'There's no tellin' what 'e is or 'e isn't likely ter do,' said Mr. Budd severely. 'You see that 'ouse-boat's kept under observation until I tell you . . . '

'Well, there's one thin', anyway,' said Leek. 'I don't s'pose 'e'll risk goin' after this other fellow, whoever 'e is.'

'I wouldn't be too sure o' that,' grunted the big man. ' 'E said 'e was goin' ter kill five people an' I believe he'll stick to 'is plan. There'll be another message to the *Clarion* before very long, you mark my words . . . '

The house phone rang and Mr. Budd glared at it.

'See who is it?' he growled, and Leek picked up the receiver.

'Cross is downstairs askin' ter see you,' he said, after listening to the message.

'Tell 'em ter shoot 'im up,' growled Mr. Budd.

Leek conveyed the message and put the receiver back on its rack.

'Wonder what 'e wants?' he said.

'I 'ope it's somethin' good,' said Mr. Budd. 'I could do with a bit o' cheerin' up.'

'So could I,' said the sergeant.

'You?' said Mr. Budd disparagingly. 'You must 'ave been born miserable. You couldn't 'ave acquired that mournful expression in thirty-seven years . . . Come in,' he added, as there was a tap on the door.

Gordon Cross was ushered into the office by a uniformed constable.

'Hello, Mr. Cross,' greeted Mr. Budd. 'If my sergeant can summon up enough energy ter get up you can 'ave that chair . . . '

'Don't worry, I'll sit on the corner of your desk,' said Gordon.

'They don't give yer very palatial

offices at the Yard,' said Mr. Budd. 'Not enough room to swing a cat — even if yer wanted to . . . What brings you 'ere?'

'I dropped in to see if you'd any news of Maurice Swayne,' said Gordon, perching himself on a corner of the desk.

'If that's what yer come for you might 'ave saved yerself the trouble,' grunted Mr. Budd.

'Meaning no, I suppose.' Gordon lit a cigarette. 'Well, that isn't all I came for. I wanted to tell you that you needn't waste your time trying to find the woman in the case. There isn't one.'

'It was only a theory o' mine,' said Mr. Budd. 'But why are you so certain there isn't?'

'Because I believe I know the motive for these murders.'

Mr. Budd sat up quickly.

'Oh, you do, eh?' he said. 'Well, I'll be very glad to hear what it is . . . '

Gordon blew out a cloud of smoke.

'I'm not ready to tell you yet,' he said.

'Now, see here, Mr. Cross,' said the big man, leaning forward, 'if you've found out the truth about this business you can't go 'andlin' it on yer own . . . '

'Oh, yes, I can,' broke in Gordon, 'and that's just what I'm going to do.'

'When I let yer in on this,' began Mr. Budd, 'you promised that . . . '

'I promised you I wouldn't publish anything without your permission. I didn't say that I'd tell you everything I discovered . . . '

'That's all very well, but . . . '

'I'm not going to freeze you out, so don't worry,' said Gordon. 'I'll hand you the solution, and the Tipster, all neatly tied up in a brown paper parcel . . . '

'D'you know who it is?' asked Mr. Budd, quickly.

'I know one of his identities: — I'm not sure, yet, of the other . . . '

'What d'yer mean — one of 'is identities?'

'You'll know — all in good time,' said Gordon. 'I promise you you shall be the first to know . . . '

'Well, that's somethin',' remarked Mr. Budd, sarcastically.

'I didn't let you down over the Bell case, did I?' said Gordon. 'You got all the credit for that, and you can have all the credit for this. All *I* want is the exclusive story for the *Clarion* . . . '

'Are you workin' for *that* rag?' asked Mr. Budd, disparagingly.

'Not now — but I shall be then . . . '

'H'm . . . ' Mr. Budd took one of his thin, black cigars from his waistcoat pocket and sniffed at it. 'When d'yer expect to 'ave this 'all neatly tied up in a brown paper parcel,' as you call it?'

'That depends,' said Gordon.

'On what?'

'On when the Tipster makes his last call,' said Gordon.

IV

'Where's my tea,' roared Mr. Tully, irritably. 'Why the blazes can't I get a cup of tea when I want it, instead of having to wait half an hour . . . '

'Sorry, sir,' said a flustered messenger boy. ''Ere you are, sir.'

'I have to expend more energy getting a cup of tea in this confounded office than I do in the make-up of the whole paper. It's ridiculous.'

'Yes, sir,' agreed the boy.

'Well, don't let it happen . . . '

'No, sir.'

'Dowling, where's Jameson?' snapped Mr. Tully, to the sub-editor.

'He hasn't come in yet, J.T.,' answered Dowling.

The News Editor of the *Clarion* gulped his tea noisily and lit a cigarette.

'When he does I suppose it'll be the same old stuff,' he grunted. 'A lot of stop-gap stuff that every other paper in the 'street' has got. When's he going to bring me something exclusive? Here we've got the greatest sensational story in years and he can't do a darned thing about it . . . Crime reporter — huh! He ought to be running Aunt Fanny's column in *Winnie's Weekly* . . . '

'Good morning, Mr. Tully,' broke in a pleasant voice. 'Can I have a word with you?'

'Who the devil are *you*?' demanded Tully.

'My name is Cross — Gordon Cross,' said Gordon.

'Who sent you up here?'

'I thought I'd find my own way up.'

'Well, you'd better find your way down again,' grunted Tully. 'I'm busy . . . '

'I wanted to see you about the Tipster,' said Gordon. 'I thought you'd be interested. However, if you feel like that about it . . . ' He turned away.

'Here, come back,' cried Tully. 'Why couldn't you say that at first?'

'You didn't give me much chance, did you?' said Gordon.

'What do you know about the Tipster?'

'How would you like the exclusive inside story for the *Clarion*, Mr. Tully?' asked Gordon.

'Have you got it?' snapped Tully.

'Not all of it — yet. I know the motive behind these murders. I shall have the identity of the Tipster very soon . . . '

'You will, eh?' Tully sounded surprised. 'That sounds fine. How do you come into it?'

'I'm a journalist — free-lance at present,' said Gordon. 'I thought there was a big story in this from the beginning . . . and I was right.'

'Got it!' Tully snapped his fingers.

'Thought I'd seen you somewhere before. You used to do the 'Courts' for the *Sentinel* . . . '

'That's right,' said Gordon. 'Well, what about it, Mr. Tully?'

'You bring me the exclusive inside story of the Tipster, properly authenticated, and I'll buy it . . . '

Gordon' shook his head.

'No, Mr. Tully,' he said.

John Tully's eyes behind his huge-shell-rimmed spectacles opened wide with astonishment.

'Eh?' he barked. 'But I thought?'

'You give me a contract as chief crime reporter on the *Clarion*, and you shall have it,' said Gordon, quietly.

'Jameson's our crime man.'

'Then you'd better get the story from him . . . '

'Now, look here, Cross . . . ' began Tully.

'Those are my terms,' said Gordon. 'You don't *have* to accept them. I've no doubt the *Sentinel* will jump at the opportunity . . . '

'We'll pay you more than the *Sentinel* . . . '

'I've told you my price, Mr. Tully,' said Gordon, firmly.

'It's nothing less than sheer blackmail,' exploded the News Editor.

'It's merely good business,' grinned Gordon. 'Well, good morning. I'll . . . '

'Don't be in such a hurry,' snapped Tully. 'I can't do anything until I've seen the Managing Editor . . . '

'Well,' said Gordon, smiling, 'Why not see him, Mr. Tully?'

John Tully shrugged his shoulders.

'All right, Cross,' he said, resignedly. 'Bring me the story and if it's all you say it is — you shall have your contract.'

'Thank you, Mr. Tully,' said Gordon.

He went back delightedly to his flat and burst in upon Vicky.

'Congratulate the *Clarion*'s new crime reporter, darling,' he said.

'Gordon, did they agree?'

'Yes — subject to my giving them the inside story of the Tipster . . . '

'Oh . . . well, you haven't got that yet,' she said.

'I will have — very soon . . . '

'If Murdoch . . . ' she began.

'Don't worry about Murdoch, darling,' he said. 'Jacob's looking after him. I rang him up and asked him if he'd go and keep an eye on Murdoch until this business is over and the old chap was delighted.'

'Is he going to stay there — at that awful place?' said Vicky.

Gordon laughed.

'The place won't worry Bellamy,' he said. 'I'll bet he's been in some worse places than that in his day.'

'Did you warn him about the fisherman?' she asked.

'Yes,' he answered. 'I wish I could have had a talk with *him*, Vicky, but by the time I'd got round to the other side of the stream he'd gone. I can't see how he comes into it . . . '

'Well, he couldn't be Henry Carrington. He's too old . . . '

'Perhaps he's somebody Carrington has employed.'

'But it was Iris Latimer we saw him with,' she said.

'I know. It's puzzling,' he said, frowning. 'You've got to allow for the fact that she may be working in conjunction with her brother . . . '

'I don't believe that, darling,' she declared.

'Or she might be working on her own. Perhaps Henry is still in Canada. She's got as much motive as he has, you know.'

'Using this man as a kind of hired thug, you mean?' she said.

'Something like that . . . '

'But that would put her completely in his power . . . '

'Seems a bit silly, doesn't it?' he admitted. 'But women have done stupider things than that before.'

'I think it's all nonsense, Gordon,' she said. 'I think Maurice Swayne is Henry Carrington. If he isn't, why has he disappeared?'

'I agree that it's more than likely. What I should like to know is — what was Lydia Kenwood looking for in Swayne's house-boat?'

'Well, *that's* not difficult,' said Vicky. 'We know that Swayne, whatever else he is, is a black-mailer . . . '

'You mean he was blackmailing Lydia Kenwood?'

'Yes, darling.'

'And she was searching for the letters, documents — whatever it is that constitutes his hold over her?' Gordon nodded thoughtfully. 'M'm ... Maybe you're right. It would account for the connection between Swayne and the Kenwoods, which always struck me as a bit queer ...'

Vicky was silent for a few minutes and then she said:

'Gordon — what's going to happen if the Tipster doesn't make an attempt on Murdoch? Supposing he leaves well alone and just fades out?'

'That,' said Gordon, 'would be a bit awkward. But I don't think there's much fear of it. There'll be no alteration in his plans — or the usual procedure — except that *this* time we know in advance *who* it's going to be.'

'Are you going to tell Mr. Budd about Martin Carrington and Murdoch?' she asked.

'No, darling,' he answered. 'I'm going to present him with a *fait accompli*. If anything leaked out, and the newspapers got hold of it, it'ud ruin my chances with the *Clarion*.'

The telephone bell rang and he lifted the receiver.

'Hello,' he called. 'Terminus 69421 . . . Hello . . . '

The line crackled faintly but there was no reply.

'Hallo,' said Gordon, impatiently, but nobody answered.

'Queer,' said Gordon, replacing the receiver. 'There's nobody there apparently . . . '

'Somebody got the wrong number, I expect, darling,' said Vicky.

'Funny they didn't *say* anything,' remarked Gordon. 'Oh, well, I suppose that's what it must have been . . . What about popping down to Carrilo's for some dinner?'

'That would be nice,' said Vicky. 'But supposing a message comes through while we're out?'

'About the Tipster?' He considered for a moment. 'I'll ring up Tully and ask him to phone me at Carrillo's . . . '

'You could do that . . . all right, I'll go and dress . . . '

'Don't be all night, darling,' said Gordon. 'I'm hungry . . . '

'I won't be more than a few minutes.' She went into the bedroom and he lit a cigarette. The telephone began to ring again and he lifted the receiver.

'Hello . . . ' he said, and a man's voice broke in.

'Is that Mr. Cross?' it said.

'Yes,' answered Gordon. 'Who?'

'This is Detective-Constable Baker, sir,' went on the voice quickly. 'Superintendent Budd asked me to telephone you. They've caught Swayne.'

'When?' demanded Gordon quickly.

'About 'alf an hour ago, sir,' said the voice. ''E was trying to get into his 'ouse-boat . . . '

'Where are you phoning from?' asked Gordon.

'The 'ouse-boat, sir. There was a bit of a scrap when we tried to take 'im and Swayne got badly 'urt. The sup'n'tendent's taking a statement from him now. He thought you might like to come along . . . '

'You bet I would,' said Gordon. 'Tell Budd I'm on my way.'

He hung up the receiver and called to his wife.

'Vicky . . . Vicky . . . '

'I'm nearly ready, darling,' she answered.

'The police have got Swayne,' he said, going into the bedroom.

'What?' cried Vicky, half in and half out of a dress.

'The fool went back to his house-boat,' said Gordon. 'He ought to have known they'd keep a watch on the place. Hurry up and finish dressing while I go and get the car . . . '

'All right,' she said. 'I'll put on another dress . . . Gordon — if Swayne is the Tipster this is going to spoil your plan, isn't it?'

He nodded.

'Yes, darling,' he answered, glumly. 'I'm afraid it is.'

V

The night was bright with moonlight. A hot, sultry night after a scorching day.

Gordon brought the car to a stop on

the towpath and opened the door.

'Here we are,' he said. 'Out you get, Vicky.'

She got out and looked across at the house-boat.

'I can't see any lights, Gordon,' she said.

'I expect the curtains are drawn,' he answered.

'They were drawn when Lydia Kenwood came here but we could still see her torch — remember?'

'Yes,' he said, staring at the dark house-boat. 'That's funny . . . '

'It looks deserted,' said Vicky, and suddenly felt frightened. 'Gordon, I — I don't like it . . . '

'Perhaps they couldn't wait for us to get here,' he suggested.

'If Swayne was very badly hurt they may have rushed him to a doctor . . . '

'I don't believe that message *was* from Mr. Budd,' said Vicky, with conviction. 'I don't believe Swayne has been caught . . . Gordon . . . let's get away from here . . . '

'I'm afraid you'll find it rather difficult,

Mrs. Cross,' said a sneering nasal voice behind them. They swung round. By the side of the car in the moonlight stood the figure of a man. His gloved hand held an ugly-looking pistol and his face was covered by a handkerchief from eyes to chin.

Vicky recognized that drawling, horrible, beastly voice and shivered.

'Oh,' she gasped. 'It's . . . it's you . . . '

'You will both do exactly as I tell you,' said the Tipster. 'This gun is not a mere melodramatic gesture. I shan't hesitate to use it . . . Get down into that boat, both of you.'

'Look here . . . ' began Gordon.

'Do as I tell you,' said the Tipster menacingly. 'I'm sure you don't want anything to happen to Mrs. Cross, do you?'

'All right.' Gordon shrugged his shoulders and went to the edge of the towpath. Moored to the bank was a small dinghy. He took Vicky's hand.

'Mind how you go, darling,' he said, as he helped her in. He got in beside her and the Tipster joined them.

'Pick up those oars and row us over to the house-boat, Mr. Cross,' he ordered.

'You'd better do as he says, Gordon,' said Vicky, as he hesitated.

'That is very sensible of you, Mrs. Cross,' said the Tipster. 'I did warn you that if your husband got too inquisitive he would find it dangerous, didn't I?'

'What . . . what are you going to do?' she asked nervously.

'Just take a necessary precaution,' he answered. 'I had to do the same thing in the case of Masters. It was unpleasant but essential.'

'Who are you?' demanded Gordon, as he pulled on the oars and sent the little boat skimming over the river.

'I prefer to conceal my identity behind this handkerchief,' said the Tipster.

'Why bother?' said Vicky. 'We know you're Maurice Swayne.'

'In that case,' he replied, 'it would appear unnecessary. I regret that your knowledge is likely to be of little use . . . '

'Don't be too sure of that — Carrington,' snapped Gordon.

'So you know *that*?' said the Tipster. 'If there had been any hope of your survival before, there is none now.'

10

I

The nose of the little boat bumped softly against the landing stage of the house-boat.

'Get out, Mr. Cross,' ordered the Tipster, 'and tie up the boat. I will follow with Mrs. Cross. Remember I have this gun and she will suffer if you try . . . '

'I know,' said Gordon. 'If it wasn't for that you wouldn't find it so easy . . . '

The Tipster laughed — it was a sound that was completely devoid of mirth.

'Now, then, Mrs. Cross,' he said, and motioned to her to get out.

Vicky got out. She stood on the wooden deck of the house-boat and watched while Gordon tied up the boat.

'What do we do next?' she asked calmly, though her heart was beating rapidly and she felt breathless with fear.

'Go into the cabin,' said the Tipster.

'The door is open — I unlocked it before you arrived . . . '

They obeyed. There was nothing else they could do. To attempt anything would have been little short of suicide.

'I'll put the light on for a few minutes,' said the Tipster, and pressed the switch inside the door. 'It will not be necessary for very long . . . '

'Supposing the police are still watching this place?' began Gordon.

'My dear Mr. Cross,' said the Tipster, 'they were — two of them . . . '

'You . . . you don't mean that you . . . ' Vicky left the sentence unfinished, staring at the masked figure in horror.

The Tipster shook his head.

'No . . . no, Mrs. Cross,' he said, 'only rendered them temporarily helpless . . . I attended to that before putting through my telephone call to your flat . . . Mr. Cross, you see that rope on the chair there?'

Gordon looked round.

'Yes,' he said.

'I shall be obliged if you will tie your wife's ankles and wrists with it . . . '

'I'll see you in hell first,' retorted Gordon.

'Don't be stupid, Mr. Cross,' said the Tipster. 'I've warned you what will happen if you don't do as you're told . . . ' He made a gesture with the pistol towards Vicky.

'All right,' said Gordon, between his teeth. He went over and picked up the rope.

'Ah, I thought you'd change your mind,' said the Tipster. 'Sit down, Mrs. Cross . . . in that chair — and put your hands behind your back . . . That's right. Now get busy, Mr. Cross, and see that you make a good job of it . . . '

Gordon set to work reluctantly. When he had finished the Tipster examined what he had done and nodded.

'Really excellent,' he remarked. 'I doubt if I could have done better myself. Now, would you mind lying down on that settee over there?'

'What for?' demanded Gordon.

'Really, Mr. Cross,' said the Tipster, 'I thought you were intelligent. Now that your wife is secure I must ensure that you are in a similar condition. I should advise you to do as I ask.'

Faced with the menace of the pistol there was only one thing to do, and Gordon did it. The Tipster made him turn over, face downwards, with his hands behind him and he felt the touch of cold steel on his wrists and heard the click of a snapping lock.

'I found these handcuffs on one of the detectives,' remarked the Tipster. 'I thought they might come in useful. Now I have only to tie your ankles and then . . . ' He paused.

'Well, go on,' said Gordon. 'What are you going to do then?'

'Wish you and Mrs. Cross — good night,' was the surprising reply.

'You mean — you're not going to . . . to . . . ?' Vicky sought for an ending to the sentence and failed to find one.

'I'm going to leave you,' said the Tipster. He stood up and surveying his handiwork: 'I don't think you'll get free from *that* in a hurry, Mr. Cross.'

'You're going to leave us here . . . just like this?' asked Gordon incredulously.

The Tipster chuckled — a horrible little cackle of suppressed laughter.

'Just like that,' he said, 'but in the dark.'

He put out the light as he spoke and went out, closing and locking the door behind him. They heard him moving about on the deck.

'Gordon,' whispered Vicky, 'do you think he's *really* gone?'

'He hasn't got in the boat yet,' said Gordon.

'Surely he wouldn't have taken all that trouble and risk just for this?' said Vicky.

'Unless he's making sure of us while he goes after Murdoch,' said Gordon.

'That might be it,' she said. 'But how did *he* know *we* knew anything about Murdoch?'

'I don't know, darling,' answered Gordon. 'Can you manage to loosen those ropes at all?'

'I'll try.' She struggled to move her hands and ankles, but the ropes wouldn't give at all. 'No,' she said breathlessly. 'You tied them too tight . . . '

'I had to,' he said. 'Listen . . . '

Faintly they heard the rattle of iron and

then the creak of the rowlocks and the ripple of water.

'He's gone,' said Gordon.

'Well, that's a relief,' said Vicky. 'I was scared to death . . . '

'So was I,' admitted Gordon. He tried ineffectually to reach the rope at his ankles with his fingers.

'We seem to be pretty effectively tied up,' he remarked. 'Are you sure you can't manage to wriggle free, darling?'

'I'll have another try,' she answered, 'but I don't . . . ' She stopped suddenly and began to sniff the air quickly.

'What are you doing that for?' he asked.

'I can smell something,' she said. 'Can't you smell something, Gordon?'

He twisted his face out of the cushions of the settee.

'No, I don't think so,' he began and then suddenly: 'Yes, I can . . . like paraffin . . . '

'Yes . . . Gordon,' she cried, and there was horror in her voice, 'there's a light under the door . . . He's . . . he's set the place on fire . . . '

'My God . . . the swine,' said Gordon,

and he felt his flesh creep. 'Vicky, you've *got* to try and get free. This place is made of wood and it must be as dry as tinder . . . The whole thing'll be ablaze in a few minutes.'

He began to strain frantically at the handcuffs. A faint crackling reached his ears and a whiff of acrid smoke wafted across his nostrils. He heard Vicky struggling somewhere behind him.

'I can't . . . shift these . . . ropes at all,' she said breathlessly.

'I'll try and roll off this settee and over to you,' he said.

By a supreme effort he managed it and fell on the floor with a bump.

'If I can get on to my knees,' he said, 'I can get over to you . . . '

Vicky coughed.

'The place is getting . . . full of smoke,' she gasped.

A tongue of flame licked up the door, flickered luridly, went out and then appeared again.

'Shout, Vicky,' said Gordon, huskily. 'Somebody may be passing on the towpath and hear you . . . '

'They couldn't get over here in time if they did,' she said, and broke into a fit of coughing.

'We can but try,' said Gordon. He began to shout for help as loudly as he could and she joined in.

The crackling of the fire was changing. An ominous roar was breaking into it and rapidly drowning it.

'The air's . . . getting . . . unbreath-able, . . . ' rasped Vicky.

'Keep on shouting,' urged Gordon, struggling towards her on his knees.

She obeyed but the smoke was filling her throat and lungs and making her cough violently. It was getting unpleas-antly hot, too.

Gordon reached her chair and began to fumble with his fingers for the knots which held her. He had to work with his back towards them and it was difficult. The perspiration began to pour down his face.

'You'll have to be quick,' gasped Vicky. 'It's getting . . . stifling . . . '

'I'm doing my best,' he croaked. 'Try shouting again, darling . . . '

'I don't . . . think I can,' she answered in a choking voice. 'My . . . throat's too . . . sore . . . '

The fire had taken hold of the wall and the curtains were blazing. The flames flickered through the swirling smoke and their shadows, grotesque and huge, danced on the opposite wall of the doomed house-boat.

Gordon's fingers were sore and he could make no headway. And all the while he worked he shouted — hoarsely and mechanically, and suddenly from outside, above the hiss and roar of the fire, came a faint answer.

'Hello . . . anybody in there?'

'Yes . . . yes,' shouted Gordon, summoning up all his strength. 'We're tied up . . . helpless . . . Can you get us out?'

There was a startled shout and a man's voice called:

'Coming . . . Hi, Speer . . . there's somebody in there . . . '

'Hurry,' shouted Gordon. 'Hurry . . . or you'll be . . . too late . . . '

The effort exhausted him. Vicky's head had dropped sideways on her shoulder and he guessed that the heat and the smoke had been too much for her.

There was a crash on the door, followed by repeated blows, and after a second or two it gave in. A man appeared dimly in the smoke and began coughing.

'Where are you?' he called, huskily.

'Here . . . ' answered Gordon, his head reeling. 'Get . . . my wife . . . out . . . She's tied to the chair and . . . she fainted . . . '

'All right,' the man answered with difficulty. 'Cripes . . . it's like a furnace in 'ere . . . Speer, give me a hand . . . '

Another man loomed up behind the first. They fought their way through the flames and smoke to Gordon's side. He could scarcely see. His eyes were streaming and painful and his lips felt cracked and dry. He must have lost consciousness for a few seconds for the next thing he knew was cool air on his face and the fire seemed to be further off . . .

'I don't think they're badly 'urt,' said a voice. ' 'Ow the 'ell did they get in there like this?'

'We'll find out when they come round,' said another voice.

'Looks darned fishy to me . . . Lord, Speer . . . there's somebody dodging among them trees . . . Get him . . . '

Gordon raised his head. The flames from the blazing house-boat lit up the trees and he saw two men struggling violently. A third man was standing near to him, watching.

'Don't let him get away, Speer,' he called.

'I've got 'im,' panted Speer. 'Now then, stop struggling, will yer?'

'Let me go,' muttered a voice huskily, and at that moment Gordon recognized the man Speer was struggling with.

'Not before we know who you are an' what you're doin' 'ere,' said Speer.

'I can tell you who he is,' said Gordon, weakly. 'His name's David Kenwood.'

II

'Give me some more tea, Gordon,' said Vicky, hoarsely. 'My throat is still sore . . . '

'Mine's like a rasp,' said Gordon. He filled two cups and gave one to his wife.

She sipped it gratefully.

They were sitting in the living-room of their flat. Mr. Budd, hastily aroused from his sleep, had come from his little house in Streatham to hear about this latest development and was ensconsced in the largest armchair, looking as though he might resume his interrupted sleep at any second. Sitting uneasily on the settee was David Kenwood.

'You're lucky to've got off with sore throats,' remarked Mr. Budd, yawning. 'If those two fellers o' mine 'adn't come to relieve the others it'd've been all up with you both. The 'ouse-boat burnt to a cinder . . . '

Vicky shuddered.

'It was dreadful,' she said.

'How did he manage to deal with the two men who were watching the place?' asked Gordon. 'The first two . . . '

Mr. Budd grunted.

'If they'd carried out their instructions,' he said, ' 'e wouldn't 'ave been able to, an' this couldn' 'ave 'appened. They ran out o' cigarettes an' Wallis went into Staines ter get some from a pub, leavin' Cobb on 'is own . . . Cobb says 'e never 'eard a sound but somethin' 'it 'im on the head an' 'e don't remember any more until he come round an' found himself trussed up with a slice o' porous plaster stuck over his mouth. The same thing happened ter Wallis when he came back with his cigarettes.'

'H'm, neat,' commented Gordon. He looked at Kenwood.

'Perhaps Mr. Kenwood can tell us more about it?' he said.

Kenwood looked startled.

'I tell you I don't know anything about all this,' he asserted. 'When I got there the house-boat was burning furiously . . . '

'What did yer go there at *all* for, Mr. Kenwood?' asked Mr. Budd.

'I just . . . I just thought I'd like to . . . to look at Swayne's house-boat,' muttered Kenwood.

'Your sister had the same idea the other night, didn't she?' said Gordon.

Kenwood moistened his lips with the tip of his tongue.

'Yes,' he answered. 'Yes, I believe she did . . . '

Mr. Budd's sleepy expression suddenly changed. He became stern and formidable.

'Now, see 'ere, Mr. Kenwood,' he snapped. 'I'm tired of listening ter fairy tales. Unless you can give me a reasonable explanation for bein' at that 'ouse-boat ter-night, I'm detainin' you on suspicion of bein' concerned with the attempted murder of Mr. and Mrs. Cross . . .'

Kenwood looked at him in alarm.

'You don't think *I'd* have anything to do with that, do you?' he demanded. 'Your own men, Wallis and Cobb, can prove that it wasn't me . . .'

'They never saw the man who attacked 'em,' said Mr. Budd.

'But — good heavens!' said Kenwood, 'it was the Tipster . . .'

'Yes,' put in Gordon meaningfully, 'it was the Tipster.'

'Well, then,' began Kenwood, and suddenly realizing what he meant: 'You don't . . . you *can't* think that I'm the Tipster?'

'We're still waitin' for your explanation,

Mr. Kenwood,' said Mr. Budd sternly.

'*I've told* you . . . '

'What were you doin' near that 'ouse-boat when Speer an' 'Owland caught yer?' persisted Mr. Budd, relentlessly.

'Mr. Kenwood,' said Vicky, 'if you had nothing to do with the fire, why don't you tell them?'

Kenwood looked from one to the other and there was a trace of desperation in his expression.

'Because,' he began, hesitantly, 'Mrs. Cross, *you* know it wasn't me.'

Vicky shook her head.

'I couldn't say who it was,' she declared. 'The Tipster wore a handkerchief over his face . . . his voice was obviously disguised . . . '

'But . . . '

'I think it was Maurice Swayne . . . '

'Of course it was Swayne,' said Kenwood.

'Why are you so sure o' that, Mr. Kenwood?' said Mr. Budd.

'That swine is capable of anything,' said Kenwood viciously.

'Do you *know* it was Swayne?' asked Gordon.

'Well, no,' answered Kenwood. 'How could I?'

'You were there too,' said Gordon.

'But I didn't get there until after the fire had started,' said Kenwood angrily. 'I keep telling you . . . '

Mr. Budd sighed.

'I'm afraid I'll 'ave to ask you to come along to the Yard,' he said. He made a movement to get up and Kenwood stopped him with a gesture.

'Wait,' he said. 'Wait. Can I have your assurance that anything I tell you will be treated strictly confidentially?'

'Well, that depends,' said Mr. Budd. 'I can't promise to withold evidence . . . '

'This has nothing to do with the Tipster,' declared Kenwood earnestly. 'It's a . . . it's a private matter . . . '

'You can rely on the fact that nothin' you tell me 'ull be made public unless it's necessary in the interests o' justice,' conceded Mr. Budd. 'That's as far as I can go . . . '

'Very well then.' Kenwood frowned for

251

a moment. 'This really concerns my sister . . . '

'Has it something to do with — blackmail, Mr. Kenwood?' asked Vicky.

'What makes you ask that, Mrs. Cross?' said Kenwood, quickly.

'I just thought that it might . . . '

'You're quite right,' he went on. 'Swayne has been blackmailing Lydia for several months . . . He managed to get hold of several letters . . . They were very indiscreet letters . . . the man they were written to is married . . . Their publication would have created a tremendous scandal.'

'So *that's* what Miss Kenwood was looking for?' said Gordon.

'Yes . . . you see Swayne kept the most important,' said Kenwood. 'I paid him several thousand pounds — my sister asked me to act for her — but he kept three letters . . . She was looking for those. You interrupted her before she could find them . . . '

'And she asked you to make another search tonight?' said Vicky.

'Yes . . . '

'Why couldn't she 'ave come out with this when I asked 'er?' demanded Mr. Budd. 'The p'lice are always ready to 'elp the victims of blackmail . . . '

'She was afraid there might be a lot of publicity,' said Kenwood.

'If only people 'ud stop 'iding up thin's . . . ' Mr. Budd shook his head sadly. 'That's what makes our job so difficult. In nine cases out of ten it's somethin' like this — somethin' they're afraid 'ull come out . . . I s'pose this is why Swayne was stayin' at that pub in Newbury?'

'Yes . . . I couldn't get rid of the man . . . '

'I s'pose people 'ull learn sense some day,' grunted Mr. Budd. 'So that's what you was doin' on that island ter-night when my men caught yer?'

'I took a boat across — lower down the river,' said Kenwood. 'I thought it would be easier to reach the house-boat that way . . . '

'You didn't see anythin' o' this Tipster feller?'

'No . . . by the time I reached the

house-boat it was already on fire.'

'Well, if the letters were there, Miss Kenwood's got nothing more to worry about,' said Gordon.

'The thing is, they weren't, Mr. Cross,' remarked Mr. Budd slowly. 'I've been through everythin' that was in the place an' if they'd been there, I'd 'ave found 'em . . . '

'That means Swayne has still got them,' said Kenwood.

'But 'e can't use 'em,' said Mr. Budd. 'So I wouldn't worry . . . '

'Do you . . . ' David Kenwood hesitated and then went on quickly: 'Do you still want me to go with you to Scotland Yard?'

'No, sir.' Mr. Budd shook his head. 'It ain't necessary now.'

'Then if you don't mind, I'll be going.' Kenwood got up. 'Good night, Mrs. Cross.'

'Good night,' said Vicky.

'I'll come with you to the door,' said Gordon.

'Don't bother,' said Kenwood. 'I can find my own way out. Good night, superintendent. Good night, Cross . . . '

He went out and they heard the front door shut and his footsteps going rapidly down the stairs.

'Well, that's cleared *that* up,' said Vicky.

'H'm,' remarked Gordon thoughtfully. 'I suppose it has . . . '

'Don't you think he was telling the truth?' she demanded.

Gordon shrugged his shoulders.

'Possibly,' he answered. 'But you know — if he *had* wanted to find a reason for being on that island to-night, it was a darned good story, wasn't it?'

III

' 'Orrible discovery in burned 'ouse-boat,' shouted the newsvendor with ghastly relish. 'Charred 'uman remains found . . . 'Orrible dis . . . paper, sir?'

'Please,' said the man who had stopped.

' 'Ere yer are, sir.' The newsboy thrust a copy of the *Daily Clarion* into his hand. The man paid his penny and as he walked away he began softly to whistle 'Clair de Lune.'

IV

Vicky, a frown wrinkling her pretty forehead, looked across the breakfast table at Gordon immersed in a copy of the *Clarion*.

'Pass me the toast, darling,' she said for the third time.

'Eh?'

'I've asked you three times for the toast, Gordon,' she said severely. 'Why don't you put down that wretched newspaper and . . . '

'Sorry, darling,' he apologized, and handed her the toast-rack.

'Tully's got it in . . . '

'Got *what* in?' she demanded.

'An account of the fire,' he answered, 'with all the gruesome details . . . charred remains . . . believed to be those of two human beings . . . That's *us*, darling.'

'Gordon!' She paused in the act of buttering a piece of toast to stare at him with wide eyes. 'Did you . . . ?'

'I 'phoned the *Clarion*,' he answered complacently. 'I want the Tipster to think he was successful . . . I don't want anything to put him off Murdoch . . . '

'But, darling . . . supposing people we *know* read that?'

'It doesn't mention anything about us by name,' he said. 'Nobody will connect *us* with it — except the Tipster.'

'I see . . . ' She nodded. 'I think that was rather bright of you, Gordon . . . '

'I have these lucid intervals occasion-ally,' he remarked.

'*Very* occasionally, darling,' said his wife. 'That's why I can't pass them without comment . . . More coffee?'

'Please.' He passed over his cup. 'I shall ignore that remark, Vicky.'

She poured out the coffee.

'Have you heard anything from Mr. Bellamy?' she asked.

'No, I don't expect to,' said Gordon. 'There's no telephone at Murdoch's and he won't leave him . . . You know, I'm a little worried. If anything should go wrong now . . . '

'You mean if the Tipster should change his plans?'

'Yes . . . I'm banking everything on him going after Murdoch . . . '

'But if he sees the account of the fire, he'll think . . . '

'That entirely depends on *who* he is, darling,' he said.

'Who?' She was puzzled for a second. 'Oh, you mean Kenwood knows the truth?'

Gordon nodded.

'I thought we'd decided that Swayne was . . . ?' she began.

'But we don't *know*,' he broke in. 'We don't know, Vicky. Besides Kenwood is very friendly with Iris Latimer. If he says anything to her, she may pass the information on . . . Whoever the Tipster is, don't forget Iris Latimer is his sister . . . '

There was a knock on the front door.

'Who the devil is that?' grunted Gordon.

'I don't know,' answered Vicky. 'Perhaps you'd better go and see, darling . . . '

'I suppose I'd better,' he said. He got

up and went out into the hall. When he opened the front door Iris Latimer was standing outside.

'Miss Latimer!' he exclaimed in surprise.

'I'm so sorry to . . . to bother you, Mr. Cross,' she said, hesitantly.

'Not at all — come in.' He recovered from his surprise. 'Vicky and I are just finishing breakfast . . . '

'I know it's awfully early,' she said apologetically.

'You mean we're awfully late,' said Gordon. He led her into the sitting-room. 'Vicky, here's Miss Latimer . . . '

'Good morning,' said Vicky.

'I must apologize for disturbing you, Mrs. Cross . . . '

'Nonsense,' said Vicky. 'Sit down, won't you? Would you like some coffee?'

'No, thank you.' Iris shook her head. 'I haven't long had breakfast myself . . . '

'Did you come all the way from Newbury?' asked Gordon.

Again she shook her head.

'No . . . no, I stayed in Town last night . . . '

She was nervous . . . Her eyes roved from one to the other. Gordon offered her a cigarette and she took it gratefully.

'I'd like one too, please, darling,' said Vicky.

He gave her one and lit them both. There was a short silence and then Iris said suddenly, as though the words had forced themselves out:

'Mr. Cross — have you seen the *Clarion* this morning?'

'I always see it every morning, Miss Latimer,' he answered.

'There's an account in it of a fire . . . a house-boat at Staines . . . '

'I thought you never read the *Clarion*?' he said.

'I never did until . . . until . . . ' She stopped.

'Until the advent of the Tipster?' he asked.

'Yes.' She inhaled deeply and slowly blew out the smoke. 'Mr. Cross . . . did — did that house-boat belong to . . . to Maurice Swayne?'

'Yes, I believe it did,' he replied.

'It says here . . . ' She touched the *Clarion*. 'It says here that . . . that some charred remains were found among the ashes . . . Is that true?'

'Why should you think *I* would know?' he asked.

'I . . . I thought, perhaps . . . the police might have told you . . . '

'They haven't mentioned it to me at all,' he said truthfully. 'But I imagine that the *Clarion* would hardly print it unless they had some basis for doing so. Is that why you came to see me?'

'Yes . . . I wondered if you . . . had any idea who — who could have been burned in the fire, Mr. Cross?'

Gordon helped himself to a cigarette and lit it carefully.

'Why are *you* so interested, Miss Latimer?' he asked.

'I was anxious . . . I thought it . . . it might have been Maurice Swayne . . . '

'The *Clarion* suggests that there was more than one person,' he said.

'Yes, I know.' She stubbed her partly-smoked cigarette out in a plate, with a nervous gesture. 'It's all very queer, Mr. Cross. Who do you think it could have been?'

'I very much doubt if Maurice Swayne was one, Miss Latimer,' he said.

'You don't think it could have been?'

'You sound relieved,' he remarked. 'Why should you be interested one way or the other?'

'It's such a horrible way to die,' she said under her breath.

'Even though it may have been the man who murdered your father?' he said.

'For . . . for *anyone*, Mr. Cross,' she said, and then suddenly: 'I must go. I have to catch the eleven-ten to Newbury . . . ' She got up. 'Will you let me know if . . . if you hear anything more?'

'Yes . . . I'll telephone you,' he said.

'Thank you so much . . . Good-bye, Mrs. Cross. Do forgive me for disturbing you like this . . . I really shouldn't . . . '

'There's no need to apologize,' said Vicky. 'You'll have to hurry if you want to catch your train . . . '

'Yes, I shall, shan't I?' She glanced at the watch on her wrist. 'Good-bye . . . Good-bye, Mr. Cross . . . '

He escorted her to the front door.

'You won't forget to let me know, will

you?' she said, as he opened it.

He promised and when she had gone, went slowly back to the sitting-room.

'Gordon — what *did* she come for?' asked Vicky.

'You heard what she said,' he answered.

'Yes — but what did she *really* come for . . . '

'We-ll.' He looked at her quizzically. 'One could almost believe that she came to find out whether that report in the *Clarion* was true . . . couldn't one?'

11

I

Mr. Budd looked up sleepily as the waitress came over to his table. He was sitting in the little tea-shop almost next door to Scotland Yard which he invariably patronized.

'A pot o' tea — nice an' strong — an' three rounds o' buttered toast, miss,' he said.

'Pot for one?' said the girl, and at that moment Mr. Budd saw the shambling figure of Leek come in and look round. 'I think yer'd better make it fer two, miss,' he said, with a sigh. 'I'm goin' ter 'ave company . . . '

The lean sergeant saw him and came over to the table.

''Ello,' he said. 'I thought I'd find yer in 'ere.'

'I'll 'ave ter try a new place,' grunted Mr. Budd. 'Further away from the Yard . . . '

264

'I won't know where ter find yer then,' said Leek.

'That,' said the big man, 'was the idea. Well, now you're 'ere, what d'yer want? Don't tell me somethin's come in?'

Leek shook his thin head and sat down.

'No, I just thought I'd like a drop o' tea,' he said.

'Oh, yer did, eh?' growled Mr. Budd.

'It's my opinion yer won't 'ear anythin' more from this Tipster feller,' remarked the sergeant.

'*That* cheers me up a lot,' said his superior. 'If you think that, we'll prob'ly 'ear from 'im at any moment . . . '

'I don't think 'e'll risk it,' said Leek, shaking his head. 'Not after that 'ouse-boat business . . . '

'I 'ope you're wrong,' remarked Mr. Budd, 'because it looks as if it was the only chance we'll 'ave of catching him . . . '

'It's a proper worry, ain't it?' sighed the sergeant.

Mr. Budd grunted. The waitress came up with the tea and the toast.

'Your friend want anything to eat?' she asked.

'No,' answered Mr. Budd, promptly. ''E's dietin' . . . '

'I wouldn't mind a bit o' cake,' said Leek.

'I'll bring you a plate of pastries,' said the girl.

'What did you want ter tell 'er that for?' demanded the aggrieved Leek, when she had gone. 'It ain't true . . . '

'You look as if it was,' said Mr. Budd, pouring out the tea.

'We can't all be fat,' said the sergeant.

'Only fat'eaded,' retorted Mr. Budd. He pushed a cup of tea across to Leek. 'I wish I knew what that feller, Cross, was up to . . . '

'Cross?' Leek raised his head. 'What's 'e bin up to?'

'Nuthin' — except get 'imself nearly killed,' said Mr. Budd, speaking with difficulty through a mouthful of toast. 'But 'e knows somethin' an' 'e's keepin' it to 'imself — somethin' about the Tipster . . . '

'You mean 'e knows who 'e is?'

'No, I don't think 'e knows that.'

'We're one up on 'im, then?'

'Yes,' said Mr. Budd. 'We know who 'e is, but not *where* 'e is . . . Is that feller Speer doin' anythin'?'

Leek shook his head.

'Put 'im on ter tail Cross,' said Mr. Budd. 'I want ter know everythin' 'e does from now on . . . '

The sergeant looked surprised.

'What good d'yer expect that'll do?' he asked.

'I've an idea it might lead us ter the feller we want . . . 'Ere are your cakes . . . '

The waitress set down a plate between them, containing two slices of indigestible-looking cake.

'Sorry,' she said, 'this is all we've got left.'

'They'll do,' said Leek. 'Thank yer, miss.'

Mr. Budd wiped his lips and got ponderously to his feet.

'I'll leave yer ter make a pig of yerself,' he said, 'an' get back to the Yard . . . My friend'll pay the bill, miss.'

' 'Ere, I say,' began Leek, but Mr. Budd ignored the protest.

'G'bye,' he called over his shoulder,

267

and waddled to the exit. As he came out into Whitehall he saw two familiar figures standing on the edge of the pavement trying to attract the attention of a passing taxi. David Kenwood and his sister.

'Damn,' grunted Kenwood, as the taxi went by.

'I don't think we're going to get one, David,' said Lydia.

'You won't very easily, miss,' remarked Mr. Budd, coming up behind them. 'This is a bad time . . . '

They both turned in surprise.

'Oh, good evening, Superintendent,' said Lydia, recognizing him.

'Good evenin',' said Mr. Budd, politely.

'We've been here for nearly ten minutes trying to get a cab,' said Kenwood, irritably.

'That's not long as thin's go these days,' said Mr. Budd. 'Where d'yer want ter go to?'

'Southampton Row,' answered Kenwood.

'There's a taxi now, David,' broke in his sister.

'Taxi . . . Hi, taxi . . . ' shouted Kenwood.

The driver slowed, swerved into the kerb and pulled up.

'You're lucky,' remarked Mr. Budd.

'Where to, sir?' asked the driver.

'Wellington Mansions, Southampton Row,' said Kenwood. He helped his sister into the cab, nodded to Mr. Budd, and the cab drove off.

Mr. Budd watched it disappear up Whitehall, and then turned into the archway to Scotland Yard.

II

'It's just along here — on the right, driver,' said David Kenwood, leaning forward and speaking through the partly open glass panel behind the driver.

The taximan nodded, and Lydia uttered a sudden exclamation.

'David, look,' she said excitedly. 'There's Maurice Swayne . . . '

'Where?' demanded Kenwood.

'There,' she said, pointing. 'Just going into that hotel . . . Look — in the check suit . . . '

'I see,' broke in Kenwood. He tapped on the glass. 'Pull up, driver, will you?'

The taxi drew into the kerb and stopped.

'You're sure it was Swayne, Lydia?' asked Kenwood.

'Yes, there's no mistaking that suit . . . '

'We ought to do something about it . . . ' Kenwood frowned. 'Swayne's wanted by the police . . . Look, Gordon Cross lives just round the corner. We'll wait for a bit and see if Swayne comes out and then we'll go and tell him . . . '

Vicky was clearing away the tea things when the knock came at the door.

'Gordon,' she called. 'See who that is, darling.'

He went to the door.

'Cross,' said Kenwood, quickly, when he opened it, 'we've just seen Swayne.'

'Swayne?' echoed Gordon. 'Where?'

'Going into a small hotel in Southampton Row,' said Lydia. 'We were in a taxi on the way to see David's solicitors . . . It's not the type of hotel one would drop in casually. He must be staying there . . . '

'Did you wait to see if he came out?'

'Yes . . . He didn't.'

'You're *sure* it was Swayne . . . ?'

'Yes, yes . . . He was wearing that loud check suit . . . The one he wore at Newbury . . . remember?'

Gordon nodded.

'I remember,' he said. 'Look here, wait just a minute, will you? I'm going to 'phone Budd. We'll get him to meet us at this hotel. I think he's as anxious to meet Mr. Maurice Swayne as I am.'

III

Mr. Budd arrived post-haste and they held a hurried consultation outside the hotel into which Maurice Swayne had been seen to vanish.

'The rest of yer 'ad better stay out 'ere,' said the big man. 'Mr. Cross an' me'll go in an' find out if 'e's there. I don't expect 'e'll be usin' 'is own name. So I'll 'ave to describe 'im. What was 'e wearing again, Mr. Kenwood?'

'Rather a big patterned check,' answered

Kenwood. 'Fawn ground with the check in fine orange lines . . . '

'That should be good enough,' said Mr. Budd. 'Come on, Mr. Cross.'

They went in through the revolving door and looked round the dingy little vestibule. In an alcove a bald-headed man was sitting behind a narrow counter reading a paper.

'We'll ask this feller,' said Mr. Budd. He walked over to the counter and the man looked up from his paper. 'I'm lookin' fer a friend,' said the big man. 'I think 'e's stayin' 'ere. 'E wears a check suit — fawn an' orange . . . '

'Oh, yes, sir,' said the man at once. 'You mean Mr. Carr?'

'That's the feller,' agreed Mr. Budd. 'What's the number of 'is room?'

'Number twelve, sir,' said the bald man. 'Shall I send up your name?'

'You needn't bother,' said Mr. Budd. 'We'll announce ourselves . . . '

'I'm afraid you can't do that, sir.' The receptionist shook his head. 'We don't . . . '

'Just take a look at this, will yer?' Mr. Budd thrust his warrant card under the other's nose. The man looked at it and his expression changed suddenly.

'You . . . you're from Scotland Yard?' he said. 'I hope there isn't going to be any trouble?'

'I 'ope so too,' said Mr. Budd. 'Number twelve you said?'

'Yes . . . first landing — on the right.' The bald man nodded towards the staircase.

'Come on, Mr. Cross,' said Mr. Budd.

They went up the shabbily carpeted stairs. From the broad landing above a corridor ran left and right and they turned into the right-hand branch. Doors that had once been white were spaced evenly along one wall, and Gordon counted the black painted numbers:

'Eight . . . nine . . . ten . . . '

'There's number twelve,' whispered Mr. Budd.

They paused outside the closed door for a moment and then the big man raised his hand and knocked. They heard movements within but the door remained closed.

Mr. Budd knocked again.

'He's in there,' whispered Gordon. 'I can hear him moving about . . . '

There was the sudden click of a latch and the door opened.

'Who is it? What do you want?' asked a voice and Gordon stared in blank amazement at the woman framed in the open doorway.

'Miss Latimer!' he ejaculated. 'I thought you'd gone back to Newbury?'

12

I

They stared at each other in mutual surprise.

'What are you doing here, Mr. Cross?' stammered Iris, after a pause.

'Surely that question applies more to *you*, Miss Latimer,' he said. 'We expected to find Maurice Swayne . . . '

'Maurice Swayne?'

'Who *is* in that room, miss?' demanded Mr. Budd.

'Nobody,' she answered. 'There's nobody there . . . '

'I'll take a look, if you don't mind,' said Mr. Budd. He walked into the small bedroom and looked about. It was empty except for themselves. He went over to the window and peered out. 'H'm,' he remarked, 'there's nobody 'ere *now*, but there's one of them very convenient fire-escapes outside this winder. Who *was*

275

'ere, Miss Latimer?'

'Nobody,' she said. She looked at him steadily. 'There's been nobody here since I came . . . Why did you say you expected to find Mr. Swayne?'

'Kenwood says he saw Maurice Swayne enter this hotel a short while ago,' said Gordon.

'*David* did?' she said quickly. 'Is *he* here?'

'He's waiting outside with his sister . . . So you didn't go back to Newbury this morning?'

'Yes . . . yes, I *did*,' she answered. 'I — I came back this afternoon . . . '

'Who did you come 'ere to see, Miss Latimer?' asked Mr. Budd, turning from an inspection of the empty wardrobe.

She hesitated.

'I . . . I came to — to see a friend,' she said, evasively.

'This room was occupied by a man who registered in the name of Carr,' said Mr. Budd. 'Was 'e the friend you come to see?'

'Yes . . . yes. That . . . that was the name . . . '

'But you didn't see 'im?'

She shook her head.

'No, I didn't. When I got here the room was empty . . . I thought I would wait for a few minutes . . . '

'With the door *locked*?'

'*I* didn't know the door was locked. It locks itself when you shut it . . . '

'I see.' Mr. Budd gently caressed his chins. 'About 'ow long did you wait?'

'About fifteen minutes, I think . . . It may have been a little longer . . . '

'The receptionist told you the number o' the room, I s'pose?'

'No. There was nobody at the reception desk when I came in. I came straight up . . . '

' 'Ow did you know which room to go to, miss?'

She was disconcerted. Her eyes flickered restlessly and she had to moisten her lips with the tip of her tongue before she could reply.

'I . . . I was told . . . ' she said and then: 'Why are you asking all these questions?'

Mr. Budd surveyed her sleepily, his fingers pinching thoughtfully at the fleshy folds of his neck.

'Because I'm very interested in this friend you came ter see, miss,' he replied slowly. 'I've every reason ter believe that 'e's the man who killed your father — the man who calls 'imself — the Tipster . . . '

She said nothing, but her face was the colour of chalk.

II

Vicky turned away from the window and looked across at her husband, lounging in an easy chair.

'The sky looks awfully black, Gordon,' she said. 'I'm sure there's going to be a storm . . . '

'Good thing, too,' he grunted. 'It'll clear the air.'

'You *know* I don't like storms,' she said.

'Well, I can't do anything about it, darling, can I?' he protested.

'You needn't sound so *pleased* . . . '

'I'm pleased at anything that'll get rid of this infernal, sticky heat,' he retorted. 'It's like a Turkish Bath . . . I wonder if

Iris Latimer did see her brother this afternoon? It's quite likely he *was* there when she arrived and left by that fire-escape when he heard us at the door . . . '

'I suppose it *was* her brother she came to see?'

'There's not much doubt about that . . . '

'Then Swayne is Henry Carrington?'

'And the Tipster.' He nodded.

'I *was* right, then — all along,' she declared.

'All along?' He laughed. 'So far as I can remember, darling, you tried everybody in turn . . . '

'Don't be silly, Gordon,' she said. 'Of course I didn't. I *always* said it was Maurice Swayne . . . '

'Well, don't let's argue about it,' he broke in hastily. 'It's quite a different matter knowing who the Tipster is and catching him . . . '

'I thought you'd got that all planned?' she said. She went back to the window and looked out.

'So I have,' said Gordon. 'But will he walk into the trap? Or will he leave well alone?'

'I think he'll make an attempt on Murdoch, if that's what you mean,' she said.

'Of course that's what I mean,' said Gordon. 'You do really think he will.'

'You don't imagine he'll give up now, do you — and leave what he started unfinished?' She picked up a cigarette from a box on the table and lit it. 'You yourself have kept on saying what a colossal vanity he's got. You don't suppose he's suddenly going to change?'

'No, I suppose not . . . ' He frowned, doubtfully. 'Something seems wrong, though, somehow . . . '

'What?'

'I don't know,' he grinned suddenly. 'Perhaps it's me. Now we're on the last lap I must be getting nervy . . . Vicky, why on earth do you keep staring out of that window?'

'Because I'm interested in something,' she replied. 'I believe somebody's watching our flat . . . '

'*What?*' Gordon jumped to his feet and came to her side.

'Look,' she said. 'Do you see that man

on the other side of the street — reading the newspaper? He's been there ever since we came in . . . '

'You're imagining things, darling,' he said, looking at the man who had roused her interest. 'He's probably only waiting for somebody . . . '

'Perhaps he is,' she said, 'but he's been waiting for a very long time. There's something familiar about him, too. I wish I could see his face . . . I'm sure I've seen him somewhere before . . . '

'Whoever it is, he's in for a wetting,' said Gordon. 'It's starting to rain . . . '

A few big drops began to fall as he spoke and the man looked up, startled. Vicky clutched her husband's arm.

'Gordon,' she exclaimed, 'it's the man who was fishing — the man Iris Latimer came to meet at the Odds On club.'

'By Jiminy, so it is,' said Gordon. 'I won't be a minute, Vicky.'

'Where are you going?' she asked, as he went quickly to the door.

'I'm going to find out who he is and what he's playing at,' he said, and was gone. He hurried down the stairs and out

281

into the street. The rain was falling more heavily now and he crossed the street quickly. The watcher looked up from his paper as Gordon stopped in front of him.

'Good evening,' he said, abruptly. 'You appear to be taking a great deal of interest in the exterior of my flat. Suppose you allow me to show you the interior?'

The man was disconcerted. He was obviously unprepared for this direct attack.

'I — I don't understand,' he stammered. 'I think you must be making a mistake, sir . . . '

'Do you?' said Gordon, pleasantly. 'Well, in any case it won't do any harm if we have a little chat, will it? You'll find it more comfortable in my flat than out here. It's beginning to rain quite heavily . . . '

'Really,' said the other, 'I don't know what you mean . . . I'm waiting for a friend . . . '

'Were you waiting for a friend when you were fishing in the Mill Stream the other day?' asked Gordon.

'I'm sure you are making a mistake . . . ' the man began.

Gordon pointed to the corner.

'There's a policeman over there,' he said. 'Perhaps you would rather talk to him?'

The man was obviously alarmed at the suggestion. His eyes flickered uneasily.

'I don't want any trouble, Mr. Cross,' he muttered.

'That's fine. Neither do I,' said Gordon. 'Let's go, shall we?'

'If you insist,' said the stranger, 'but I assure you that this is all a misunderstanding . . . '

'Then it's time we cleared it up, isn't it?' said Gordon. 'I see you know my name, which rather gives you the advantage?'

'My name is Gates — Simon Gates,' said the man, quickly, taking the hint.

'Ah, that's better,' said Gordon. 'Now we're on more equal terms.'

He led the way across the street and into the vestibule of the flats. In silence they mounted the stairs side by side. Outside the front door Gordon produced his key and put it in the lock.

'Here we are, Mr. Gates,' he said. 'In you go . . . '

The man who called himself Simon Gates went in. Gordon shut the door and ushered him into the sitting-room.

'Vicky,' he said, 'this is Mr. Simon Gates. We're going to have a nice, cosy little chat. Mr. Gates — my wife . . . '

The man bowed awkwardly.

'How do you do, ma'am,' he said. 'I'm afraid there's a . . . '

'Do sit down,' said Vicky. 'You must be tired after standing out there for such a long time . . . '

'Thank you, ma'am, but I . . . ' began Mr. Gates.

'Try this chair,' Gordon pushed forward a chair behind the man's knees and he sat down rather hurriedly. 'Now, Mr. Gates — *who are you?*'

'I've told you . . . '

'But not enough,' went on Gordon, shaking his head. 'Not *nearly* enough. I want to know a great deal more about you than your name — always supposing it *is* your name . . . '

'I assure you, Mr. Cross, that you are under a misapprehension,' began Gates earnestly.

'Well, if I am,' Gordon interrupted, 'this little talk will clear it up, won't it?' His voice changed from its light, bantering tone. 'About a year ago I happened to be in a London police court. I was working for the *Sentinel* — a newspaper you may have heard of . . . A man was brought up and charged with severely wounding two other men in a street off Soho. Do you remember that, Mr. Gates?'

'Well, I . . . ' Gates fumbled for his words. 'Yes . . . I . . . '

'That man was *you*,' said Gordon. 'I don't know the result of the case — I had to leave the court temporarily before it was concluded . . . '

'That was a pity, Mr. Cross,' said Gates. 'If you had stayed you would have heard me discharged. Self-defence is not a crime . . . '

'So that's your explanation?' said Gordon. 'These men set upon you and you merely defended yourself. Is that it?'

Gates smiled slightly.

'That's it, Mr. Cross,' he said.

'Well,' said Gordon, 'now will you kindly explain what the connection is between you and Iris Latimer?'

Gates shook his head.

'That is a different matter, Mr. Cross,' he said. 'It concerns only Miss Latimer and myself.'

'You think so?' Gordon looked at Vicky. 'Darling, ring up Scotland Yard and ask for Superintendent Budd, will you?'

She got up and went over to the telephone.

'Here, just a minute,' exclaimed Gates, in alarm. 'I don't want the police dragged into this . . . '

'There'll be no need to *drag* them, I assure you,' said Gordon. 'They'll come at the double. However, if you've changed your mind, perhaps it won't be necessary . . . '

'You're placing me in a very awkward position, Mr. Cross,' said Gates. 'Anything that takes place between myself and my clients is, naturally, regarded as confidential . . . '

'Clients?' Gordon raised his eyebrows.

Simon Gates took a card from his pocket and held it out.

'Here is my card,' he said. 'I think it

will explain what I mean.'

Gordon glanced at the card. Inscribed in neat copperplate he read: *Simon Gates, Private Inquiry Agent.*

'Ah, now I understand,' he said, his face clearing. 'Miss Latimer consulted you professionally?'

Gates nodded.

'Yes,' he answered. 'She asked me to trace the present whereabouts of her brother . . . '

'Henry Carrington who went to Canada when he was fifteen?' broke in Gordon, and the private detective looked surprised.

'You *know* that, Mr. Cross?' he said.

'I probably know a lot more than you think,' said Gordon. 'Were you successful?'

'Only up to a point,' said Gates. 'My agent in Canada succeeded in tracing him to a nursing home near Ontario, in which he was confined for three years . . . '

'A nursing home?' interrupted Vicky. 'Do you mean an asylum?'

'Well, something of a very similar nature, Mrs. Cross,' admitted Gates. 'He escaped eighteen months ago and since then all trace of him appears to have vanished . . . '

'Why did they — shut him up?' she asked.

'Well, apparently the boy was a very sensitive youngster,' said the detective. 'He'd almost worshipped his father and he brooded over his death — kept all the newspaper cuttings about it — and seems to have got it fixed in his head that his father was murdered. It became a mania with him as he grew older . . . '

'Was that why they had to put him into an asylum?' asked Vicky.

'Yes. He attacked a man who taunted him with being the son of a crook and nearly killed him. The report says that except for this obsession he was outwardly normal and very intelligent . . . '

'It's . . . rather sad, Gordon, isn't it?' she said.

'Yes,' said Gordon. 'Because you know he was right in a way. Morally those four men *were* guilty of killing his father.'

'Did Miss Latimer think that her brother was the Tipster, Mr. Gates?' said Vicky.

'She never actually *said* so, Mrs. Cross,' he replied, 'but, well, after she'd told me the story, I guessed that was in her mind. It was obvious.'

'I feel awfully sorry for her,' she said.

'Yes — a horrible position to be in,' said Gordon. 'Do you know whether her brother was *aware* that she had been adopted by Latimer?'

'According to what Miss Latimer told me, he couldn't have been,' said Gates. 'It happened after he'd gone to Canada. She told me that Lord Latimer had expressly forbidden any communication between them. He wished her to regard *him* as her only relative.'

'H'm . . . natural, I suppose, if he was bringing her up as his own daughter,' said Gordon.

'Couldn't you find any trace of him at all?' said Vicky.

'None at all, Mrs. Cross,' answered Gates. 'Of course it was quite certain that he must be the Tipster. Miss Latimer must have realized *that*. Her great anxiety, I think, was to find him and stop him committing any more crimes. Unfortunately she couldn't help me very much. You see, she hadn't seen her brother since she was seven years old and she had no idea what he was like.'

'He was at the Vendome Hotel in Southampton Row, Mr. Gates,' said Gordon. 'Miss Latimer was there too. Whether they met, I don't know.'

'I didn't know about that,' said Gates quickly. 'How did she know he was there?'

'That I couldn't tell you,' said Gordon.

'She came to see me early this morning — after she'd read that account in the *Clarion* of the fire at Swayne's houseboat,' said Gates. 'She seemed to think that the remains might have been her brother's . . . '

'Gordon — that's why she was so interested,' cried Vicky.

'George Murdoch was one of the people who had been involved in the father's death,' said Gates, 'and I kept a watch on him for some time, hoping Carrington might put in an appearance. I shouldn't have known him, of course, but if anybody had turned up there it was my intention to follow them and find out all about them. Nobody did,' he added, ruefully, 'except you and Mrs. Cross.'

'Why were you keeping a watch on this flat?' asked Gordon. 'Were you expecting Carrington would turn up here?'

'Well — no, not exactly, Mr. Cross,' said Gates, smiling. 'To be quite candid I was keeping a watch on *you*.'

'On me?' echoed Gordon. 'You're not suggesting that I'm the Tipster, are you?'

'No, but I thought perhaps you might lead me to him. You obviously knew about Murdoch and therefore you must have found out the connection with Carrington . . . '

'I see,' Gordon nodded, thoughtfully. 'Well, that seems to explain your share in this business . . . '

'I hope you'll treat what I have told you in strict confidence, Mr. Cross,' said Gates. 'You can understand, now, why I didn't want the police brought into it. I wouldn't like Miss Latimer to think . . . '

'Don't worry, Mr. Gates, I shan't say anything,' said Gordon. 'Well, I don't think we need detain you any longer . . . '

The private detective was only too anxious to go. Gordon saw him to the door and came back to the sitting-room.

'Well, darling,' he said, cheerfully, 'that clears *that* up.'

'Yes,' replied Vicky. 'All we've got to do now is to find the Tipster.'

And at that exact moment the telephone bell began to ring.

Gordon lifted the receiver and John Tully's voice spoke in his ear — urgently and with suppressed excitement.

'The Tipster's just come through, Cross,' he said. 'Says it's his last message . . . '

'And the name's George Murdoch,' broke in Gordon.

'How did you know that?' Tully's voice was astonished.

'I know everything now, Mr. Tully,' said Gordon, 'except the identity of the Tipster. I expect to know that — to-night.'

III

'*Patrol car FX5. Patrol car FX5 calling Information Room, calling Information*

292

Room. Detective-Constable Speer report-
ing. Cross just left his flat with Mrs.
Cross in car. Heading south. Over.'

'Information Room calling Patrol car
FX5. Information room calling Patrol car
FX5. Keep Cross's car in sight. Notify
direction and whereabouts to Patrol car
QS9. Over.'

'Patrol car FX5 calling Information
Room. Patrol car FX5 calling Information Room. Contacting Patrol car QS9,
Patrol car QS9 as instructed. Cutting
out. Patrol car FX5 calling Patrol car QS9.
Patrol car FX5 calling Patrol car QS9. Are
you receiving me? Over.'

'Patrol car QS9 calling Patrol car FX5.
Patrol car QS9 calling Patrol car FX5.
Receiving you clearly. Follow car containing Cross and keep us notified of your
whereabouts.'

IV

The storm which had been threatening
broke suddenly in a deluge of rain and
the almost incessant crash of thunder.

293

The crazy old structure of the Mill House shook under the fury of the wind and Murdoch, slumped in a chair in the dirty living-room, stirred uneasily.

Old Jacob Bellamy, a cigar in the corner of his mouth, sat on the other side of the table. A peal of thunder crashed almost overhead and Murdoch started so violently that he nearly fell out of his chair.

'What's the matter with yer, cock?' demanded Bellamy. 'You're as jumpy as a kangaroo . . . '

'It's this storm,' grunted Murdoch. 'I allus 'ated 'em . . . '

'Cor blimey, you're worse than a kid,' said Bellamy contemptuously.

Murdoch passed a dirty hand across his face.

'I keep 'earing thin's,' he muttered uneasily. 'Footsteps outside . . . '

'You'd better pull yerself together . . . '

'You 'aven't got this feller after yer, 'ave yer?' said Murdoch hoarsely. 'It's all very well for *you* to talk . . . '

' 'E can't 'urt yer now I'm 'ere,' said Bellamy confidently.

'What about them other blokes?' said Murdoch.

'They didn't 'ave *me* looking after 'em,' retorted old Jacob. 'Nobody ain't got the better of old Jacob Bellamy yet. I've bin up against some toughs in me time an' they've always got the worst of it. You ask any of the 'wide' boys . . . '

'That's different,' said Murdoch. 'This man's . . . '

He stopped abruptly as an urgent knocking came on the door and echoed through the old building.

' 'Oo's that?' Murdoch half started to his feet.

'Sit down,' ordered Bellamy. 'I'll go and see.'

'Don't you open the door,' said Murdoch.

'Keep quiet an' leave it ter me, cock,' growled Bellamy, and went out into the passage, his footsteps thudding on the bare boards. Before he pulled the bolts that secured the crazy door, the old man drew an automatic from his pocket and thumbed back the safety catch. Cautiously he opened the door an inch.

'Who's there?' he demanded.

'It's only us, Jacob — Vicky and me,' said Gordon Cross. 'You can put that gun away . . . '

'Come on in, cock,' said Bellamy, opening the door wide. 'Blimey! What a night, ain't it?'

'Beastly,' said Vicky, her raincoat dripping streams of water on the dirty floor. 'My shoes are soaking.'

Bellamy shut the door and re-bolted it.

'We left the car in a clump of trees,' said Gordon, wiping his wet hair with a handkerchief. 'We didn't want to advertise our presence. Anything happened, Jacob?'

'Not a ruddy thing, boy,' replied Jacob Bellamy. 'Everythin' as quiet as a Victorian Sunday afternoon in Tootin' . . . '

'It won't be for long,' said Gordon. 'The Tipster telephoned the *Clarion* this evening . . . '

'So we can expect 'is nibs at any moment, eh, cock?' The old man rubbed his hands. ' 'E's chosen a nice night for it, ain't 'e?'

A peal of thunder went rolling and echoing overhead and the windows all lit with a vivid blue glare.

'Do you mean 'e's on 'is way 'ere *now*,' demanded Murdoch apprehensively.

'Yes — but you needn't worry yourself,' said Gordon. 'Nothing's going to happen to you.'

'That's all very well,' muttered Murdoch, 'but 'ow d'yer know?'

'Now just you shut up an' leave it to us,' said Bellamy.

'How long do you think we shall have to wait?' asked Vicky.

'Probably not very long,' answered Gordon. 'I think he'll bank on the fact that it will take us some time to locate Murdoch's whereabouts, and get here soon after dark. He'll think that there'll be plenty of time to finish what he came for and get away before the police or anybody can arrive. It won't occur to him that we knew about Murdoch *before* he put his call through . . . '

'We'll 'ope so, anyway,' said Bellamy. He went to a cupboard and brought back glasses and a bottle of John Haig. 'What about a spot o' Scotch before the fun starts, eh?'

'That,' said Gordon, with enthusiasm,

'is a very good idea, Jacob.'

The old man poured out the drinks.

''Ark at it,' he said, as another crash of thunder shook the house. 'Like bein' back in the old air raids, ain't it?'

'I hate thunder storms,' said Vicky. 'They scare me . . . '

'An' me,' muttered Murdoch.

'They can't do yer no 'arm,' said Bellamy. 'Not unless yer gets in the way of a bit o' lightning . . . '

''Ere — wot about me?' growled Murdoch, eyeing the bottle of whisky longingly. 'Can't I 'ave a drink?'

' 'Course you can, cock,' said Bellamy. He splashed some whisky into a glass and pushed it across the table. 'There yer are — knock that back. What d'yer think this feller'll do when 'e gets 'ere?'

'I think he'll come to the door and knock in the ordinary way,' said Gordon. 'He'll expect to find Murdoch alone . . . '

'What do we do?' asked the old man.

'We creep along the passage and take up our positions on either side of the door,' said Gordon. 'Then we open it and grab him.'

'As easy as kiss yer 'and,' said Bellamy.

'For goodness' sake be careful,' said Vicky, anxiously. 'Don't forget you'll be dealing with a crazy man . . . '

'I'm not forgetting it, darling,' said Gordon. 'I'm counting on taking him by surprise.'

'I'll feel much happier when it's all over,' she said.

'So'll I,' said Murdoch. 'It's all very well for you, but this chap's after *me*. S'pose sump'n goes wrong? S'pose 'e gets in . . . '

'That'll be just too bad for all of us, cock,' grunted Bellamy.

'Don't talk so loud,' warned Gordon. 'This old place isn't sound-proof . . . '

'You don't think he's — he's lurking outside *now*?' asked Vicky.

'We can't tell,' said Gordon. 'It's just as well to take precautions . . . '

'Gordon,' she interrupted, as a thought struck her, 'supposing he got here first and saw us arrive . . . '

'We've got to take a chance on that,' he said.

'''Ere, give me another drink, will you?'

said Murdoch. 'I . . . '

'Listen!' whispered Vicky suddenly.

'What is it?' asked Gordon.

'I thought I heard something — outside,' she whispered.

They listened tensely, but there was no sound except the hiss and drumming of the rain.

'I can't hear anything,' whispered Gordon. 'What . . . ?'

'Be quiet,' said Vicky impatiently.

A sound reached them now — the faint creak of the gate's rusty hinge.

'Somebody's opening the gate,' said Vicky. They almost held their breaths, but now there was only the rain.

'Perhaps it was the wind . . . ' began Gordon, but his wife silenced him with a gesture. Faintly at first but growing louder came the sound of somebody whistling 'Clair de Lune'.

'It wasn't the wind.' Vicky breathed the words so that they were only just audible. They heard the crunch of footsteps on wet gravel and the plaintive melody of 'Clair de Lune' grew louder still.

'He's coming,' whispered Gordon. 'Get

down to the door, Jacob — quietly . . . '

They tiptoed out of the living-room and along the passage to the front door. As they took up their positions on either side of the door the footsteps outside came right up to the porch and stopped. There was a moment's silence and then a knock.

'Now,' whispered Gordon.

Bellamy drew back the bolts and opened the door. As he did so there was a tremendous crash of thunder and a searing flash of lightning that lit up the wet path and dripping bushes and trees brighter than noonday.

There was nobody there.

Bellamy uttered an oath and was stepping across the threshold when Gordon caught his arm.

'Don't go outside,' he said. 'He may be lurking . . . '

From behind them came a sudden crash of breaking glass and a woman's scream.

'That's Vicky,' cried Gordon. 'The window . . . '

They ran back along the passage and

into the living-room.

'Gordon . . . Gordon,' cried Vicky. 'He's here . . . '

Framed in the broken window was the head and shoulders of a man. In one hand he held an automatic and his face was covered by a dark handkerchief.

'Don't move, any of you.' The sneering, nasal voice was unmistakable. 'Unless you keep quite still — exactly where you are — I shall shoot Mrs. Cross . . . My sudden appearance at the window rather disconcerted you all, didn't it? You expected to find me at the door. I always endeavour to do the unexpected . . . '

'It didn't work at the house-boat, did it?' said Gordon.

'Apparently not, Mr. Cross,' said the Tipster, 'though I quite thought it had when I saw the account in the *Clarion*. That was clever of you . . . '

'Thanks,' said Gordon.

'But not quite clever enough — as you see . . . '

'If you think you're going to get away with this,' began Gordon.

'I shall, Mr. Cross,' interrupted the

Tipster. 'There's really nothing you can do to stop me — unless, of course, you are prepared to sacrifice your wife's life. I shall carry out what I came here to do and then vanish into the darkness, my task completed. The Tipster — a rather appropriate pseudonym, don't you think, if a trifle melodramatic? — will disappear for good . . . '

'And who will he become?' asked Gordon.

'Just an ordinary citizen, Mr. Cross,' replied the man at the window. 'I prefer a quiet life. In this matter you must realize that I have only been the instrument of justice. The law could not touch these men who were responsible for my father's death. I took the place of the law.'

'Nobody has a right to do that, Carrington,' said Gordon quietly.

'I'm afraid I must differ with you, Mr. Cross,' replied the Tipster.

'*Latimer* only did his duty, Carrington,' said Gordon. 'And he was kind to your sister — he adopted her after you went to Canada . . . gave her every care and affection . . . '

'Yes,' said the Tipster. 'I only found that out yesterday — I wish I'd known before . . . '

'You telephoned her asking her to come and see you at that hotel in Southampton Row, didn't you?'

'You appear to know a great deal, Mr. Cross,' said the Tipster. 'Yes, I did, but I realized that Kenwood saw me going in . . . '

'So you left by the fire-escape without seeing her?'

'It was a question of discretion being the better part of valour,' said the Tipster.

'Then you are . . . you *are* Maurice Swayne?' breathed Vicky.

'Yes . . . yes, Mrs. Cross. I am Maurice Swayne . . . '

'I knew it,' she cried. 'I was sure . . . '

'I cannot afford to waste any more time,' he said impatiently. 'Stand up, Murdoch.'

Murdoch cringed back in his chair, his eyes starting in terror.

'No,' he whined. 'No, no, no . . . Yer can't . . . I only did what Tidmann told me . . . '

'Stand up,' said the Tipster, curtly.

'Carrington,' said Gordon. 'Think what you're doing . . . '

'Stand up,' ordered the Tipster, ignoring his interruption.

'I won't.' Murdoch's face was desperate and dewed with sweat. 'You've got ter listen ter me . . . I didn't do nuthin' . . . '

'Then die where you are,' snarled the Tipster, and his finger tightened on the trigger. There was a flash and a report. Murdoch uttered a strangled cry and half rose. Then he fell against the table and collapsed on the floor, writhed for a moment groaning and lay still.

'You've . . . killed him,' whispered Vicky, her face white.

'That was my object in coming here,' said the Tipster. 'Now I can go . . . '

A whistle shrilled out faintly behind him and a voice — Gordon recognized it at once — called urgently: 'There 'e is — at the winder . . . Spread out an' we'll get 'im . . . '

'That's Budd,' cried Gordon.

The Tipster disappeared from the shattered window and they heard the sound of confused shouting outside, followed by a succession of shots.

'Come on, Jacob,' said Gordon, and raced for the door with Vicky and Bellamy at his heels. He wrenched open the door and dashed out into the wet darkness. The lights of electric torches were moving and gleaming like fire-flies and Mr. Budd's voice reached him from some distance away: ' 'E's makin' for the old mill-wheel . . . Leek . . . Leek!'

' 'Ello?' answered Leek faintly.

'Stop 'im,' shouted Mr. Budd. ' 'E's goin' ter try an' cross the stream . . . If 'e gets over we may lose 'im . . . '

Somebody switched on the headlights of a car and they blazed through the darkness like twin searchlights, flooding the old mill-wheel with light.

'Look . . . oh, look,' cried Vicky. 'He's climbing up over the mill-wheel . . . '

'The fool,' said Gordon. 'It'll never hold his weight. The whole thing's rotten . . . '

Even as he spoke there came a splintering crack. They saw the figure of the Tipster sway, clutch frantically at one of the paddles of the wheel, and then, as it broke in his grasp, fall backwards into the weed-covered water.

''E's fallen in the stream,' shouted Mr. Budd. 'Get 'im out, some of yer . . . '

Leek and another man waded in. The water was very shallow, reaching only up to their ankles. Presently they came out carrying something which they laid on the bank.

'I think 'e's dead,' said Leek, as they came up to him. 'There's a 'eap o' stones there an' 'e smashed 'is 'ead on 'em when 'e fell . . . '

'H'm,' remarked Mr. Budd. 'Let's 'ave a look.' He bent down. 'Yes, 'e's dead all right.' He straightened up. 'Well, there's the Tipster, Mr. Cross. Want ter see who 'e was?'

'We know, Mr. Budd,' said Vicky. 'Maurice Swayne.'

'You do, eh?' said the big man. 'I think you'd better take a *look*, Mrs. Cross . . . '

She hesitated, and then went over and stooped above the thing on the bank.

'Oh!' She gasped with a sudden quick-drawn breath. 'It . . . it *can't* be . . . '

It was Masters who lay there.

'It is, Mrs. Cross,' said Mr. Budd, mopping his face. 'Yer see, the man who was killed in that quarry at Newbury was Maurice Swayne . . . '

13

I

'Have another drink, Vicky?' said Gordon.

'Are you trying to make me tight, Gordon Cross?' she demanded.

He laughed.

'What does it matter, darling?' he said. 'This is a celebration, isn't it? Waiter.'

'Yes, sir?'

'Double Gordon's gin and orange with ice and a little soda,' ordered Gordon, 'and a double whisky and ginger-ale . . . '

'Yes, sir.' The waiter hurried away and Gordon leaned back in his chair and looked contentedly round the Odds On club. He was thoroughly enjoying himself. Jacob Bellamy came across the dance floor and joined them, a broad grin on his weather-beaten face.

' 'Ello, cock,' he greeted. ' 'Avin' a good time? You look very nice, m'dear.'

'Thank you, Mr. Bellamy,' said Vicky.

'Gordon's celebrating.'

'So 'e ought,' said the old man. 'That was a jolly good story, cock, 'exclusive ter the *Clarion* by Gordon Cross.' I'll bet you thought that looked good, eh?'

'Sit down, Jacob, and have a drink,' said Gordon. 'Budd said he'd drop in later . . . '

'Kenwood rang up ter book a table for three, a couple o' hours ago,' said Bellamy. 'So it looks as if it 'ud be quite a family gatherin'.'

'Is he bringing his sister and Iris Latimer with him?' asked Vicky.

'I s'pose so,' answered Bellamy. 'She took it very well, poor kid, didn't she? — the death of 'er brother.'

'Well, she never really knew him, did she?' said Gordon. 'He was practically a stranger to her.'

'It must have been a relief, I should think,' said Vicky. 'You know, it's queer that he should have been butler there for over a year and they never realized they were brother and sister . . . '

'Not so queer really,' said Gordon. 'There was no reason why they should.

They hadn't seen each other since they were children.'

'So that feller Swayne really *did* see the murderer on the night Masters killed Latimer, eh, cock?' remarked Bellamy.

Gordon nodded.

'Of course,' he said. 'That's why he picked out 'Clair de Lune' on the piano when he called the next day, to let Masters *know* that he knew. Blackmail was Swayne's speciality, but he tried to blackmail the wrong sort of person with Masters. Masters made an appointment to pay him off at the quarry, killed him, changed clothes with him, and then battered his face and head to pulp with that stone, so he'd be unrecognizable. The reason he rang me up that day was to provide a motive for his own, apparent, murder.'

'It didn't work,' grunted Bellamy. 'Budd knew it wasn't Masters who was killed all the time, so 'e says.'

'Yes, but he wanted Masters to *think* his plan *had* succeeded, so he didn't say anything to anybody,' said Gordon. 'I've a bone to pick with him over *that*.'

311

'*You* can't say much, cock,' commented Bellamy. 'You didn't tell 'im all yer knew, did yer?'

'When we saw Swayne in that wood — after Crawford was killed,' interrupted Vicky, 'he was following Masters, I suppose?'

'Yes, and the note that was found in Crawford's pocket was written to *Masters* by *Swayne*, making an appointment at Newbury. Masters put it in Crawford's pocket for the same reason he wiped the knife on Lydia Kenwood's handkerchief — to confuse the issue. She must have dropped it sometime when she was over at the Latimers' . . . '

'How was Mr. Kenwood able to tell that the note Masters sent to Iris Latimer after Swayne's death had been typed on Swayne's machine?' asked Vicky.

'Obviously because he'd had a number of notes from Swayne, himself,' said Gordon. 'Swayne was blackmailing Lydia Kenwood, wasn't he? That's what brought him to Newbury in the first place. Kenwood told us he was dealing with him for her. That's why he went so white when Swayne turned up at the Latimers' . . . '

'I wonder what happened to those letters, Gordon,' said Vicky.

'I think they were burned in the fire,' he answered. 'Swayne wouldn't have left them lying about. He probably kept things like that in a secret hiding place . . . ' He broke off. 'There are the Kenwoods now,' he went on, 'with Iris Latimer . . . and, by Jove, Budd, too . . . '

The waiter came up with a tray of drinks.

'Gin and orange, sir,' he said, 'whisky and ginger-ale . . . '

'Bring a large Scotch for Mr. Bellamy and some beer, will you?' said Gordon.

'Yes, sir.'

''Ello, Mr. Cross,' greeted Mr. Budd, coming ponderously up to the table. 'Good evenin', Mrs. Cross. This sort o' thin' isn't much in my line, but I thought I'd just pop in an' congratulate yer 'usband . . . 'Ow d'yer do, Mr. Bellamy?'

'Wotcher, cock,' said old Jacob.

'Sit down, Budd,' said Gordon, 'I've ordered some beer . . . '

'That sounds good to me,' said Mr.

Budd. He sank heavily into a chair. 'That was a good story yer printed in the *Clarion*, Mr. Cross. The photergraph o' me wasn't too flatterin', though . . . Looking at that people 'ud think I was fat . . . '

'And they'd be right,' said Gordon.

'I was right all along,' broke in Vicky. 'I always said it was Masters, didn't I, Gordon?'

'Well, darling,' said Gordon, 'need we go into that?'

'Hello, Cross,' said David Kenwood, coming over. 'I say, bring your party over to our table and join us, will you? Iris and I have just got engaged and we'd like you all to drink our health . . . '

'It took him such a long time to screw up his courage and ask her,' broke in Lydia, 'but he did it at last.'

'Congratulations,' said Gordon.

'Order what yer like, Mr. Kenwood,' said Bellamy. 'Everythin's on the 'ouse . . . '

'That's very nice of you, Mr. Bellamy,' said Kenwood.

'It's a pleasure, cock,' said the old man.

'*I* think it's sweet of you,' said Iris.

'Gordon,' said Vicky, with conviction,

'I'm *sure* you'll have to carry me home . . . '

'Mr. Cross?' A waiter came hurrying up.

'Yes?' said Gordon.

'There's a telephone message for you, sir,' said the man. 'From a Mr. Tully. He says will you go to the offices of the *Daily Clarion* at once. It's very urgent . . . '

'Oh, heck!' groaned Gordon.

'Gordon — you're not going to leave me here?' began Vicky.

'Sorry, darling,' he said, getting up. 'I'm afraid I'll have to . . . '

'What d'they want yer for, cock?' asked Bellamy.

Gordon shrugged his shoulders.

'I don't know,' he said. 'You'd better get the *Clarion* and find out. Look after my wife, Budd, will you? If she becomes drunk and disorderly, lock her up and I'll come and bail her out in the morning.'

THE FACELESS ONES
GRIM DEATH
MURDER IN MANUSCRIPT
THE GLASS ARROW
THE THIRD KEY
THE ROYAL FLUSH MURDERS
THE SQUEALER
MR. WHIPPLE EXPLAINS
THE SEVEN CLUES
THE CHAINED MAN
THE HOUSE OF THE GOAT
THE FOOTBALL POOL MURDERS
THE HAND OF FEAR
SORCERER'S HOUSE
THE HANGMAN
THE CON MAN
MISTER BIG
THE JOCKEY
THE SILVER HORSESHOE
THE TUDOR GARDEN MYSTERY
THE SHOW MUST GO ON
SINISTER HOUSE
THE WITCHES' MOON
ALIAS THE GHOST
THE LADY OF DOOM

THE BLACK HUNCHBACK
PHANTOM HOLLOW
WHITE WIG
THE GHOST SQUAD
THE NEXT TO DIE
THE WHISPERING WOMAN
THE TWELVE APOSTLES
THE GRIM JOKER
THE HUNTSMAN
THE NIGHTMARE MURDERS

With Chris Verner:
THE BIG FELLOW
THE SNARK WAS A BOOJUM

We do hope that you have enjoyed reading this large print book.

Did you know that all of our titles are available for purchase?

We publish a wide range of high quality large print books including:
Romances, Mysteries, Classics
General Fiction
Non Fiction and Westerns

Special interest titles available in large print are:
The Little Oxford Dictionary
Music Book, Song Book
Hymn Book, Service Book

Also available from us courtesy of Oxford University Press:
Young Readers' Dictionary
(large print edition)
Young Readers' Thesaurus
(large print edition)

For further information or a free brochure, please contact us at:
Ulverscroft Large Print Books Ltd.,
The Green, Bradgate Road, Anstey,
Leicester, LE7 7FU, England.
Tel: (00 44) **0116 236 4325**
Fax: (00 44) **0116 234 0205**

Other titles in the
Linford Mystery Library:

STING OF DEATH

Shelley Smith

Devoted wife and mother Linda Campion is found dead in her hall, sprawled on the marble floor, clutching a Catholic medallion of Saint Thérèse. An accidental tumble over the banisters? A suicidal plummet? Or is there an even more sinister explanation? As the police investigation begins to unearth family secrets, it becomes clear that all was not well in the household: Linda's husband Edmund — not long home from the war — has disappeared; and one of their guests has recently killed himself . . .